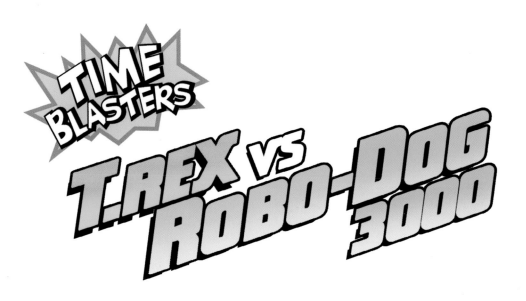

TIME BLASTERS

T. REX VS ROBO-DOG 3000

Librarian Reviewer
Katharine Kan
Graphic novel reviewer and Library Consultant, Panama City, FL
MLS in Library and Information Studies, University of Hawaii at
Manoa, HI

Reading Consultant
Elizabeth Stedem
Educator/Consultant, Colorado Springs, CO
MA in Elementary Education, University of Denver, CO

STONE ARCH BOOKS
www.stonearchbooks.com

Graphic Sparks are published by Stone Arch Books
151 Good Counsel Drive, P.O. Box 669
Mankato, Minnesota 56002
www.stonearchbooks.com

Library of Congress Cataloging-in-Publication Data
Nickel, Scott.
T. rex vs Robo-Dog 3000 / by Scott Nickel; illustrated by Enrique Corts.
p. cm. — (Graphic Sparks.Time Blasters)
ISBN 978-1-4342-0761-6 (library binding)
ISBN 978-1-4342-0857-6 (pbk.)
1. Graphic novels. [1. Graphic novels. 2. Time travel—Fiction. 3. Robots—Fiction. 4. Tyrannosaurus rex—Fiction. 5. Dinosaurs—Fiction.] I. Corts, Enrique, ill. II. Title. III. Title: Tyrannosaurus rex versus Robo-dog three thousand.
PZ7.7.N53Ty 2009
[Fic]—dc22 2008006714

Summary: David's brother, Darrin, just invented a radio-controlled pooch. It performs tricks, mixes delicious smoothies, and grows 50 feet tall. When David's friend brings back a T. rex from the past, Robo-Dog 3000 turns into the ultimate fighting machine. It's beast versus bot in the smackdown of the century!

Art Director: Heather Kindseth
Graphic Designer: Brann Garvey

1 2 3 4 5 6 13 12 11 10 09 08

Printed in the United States of America

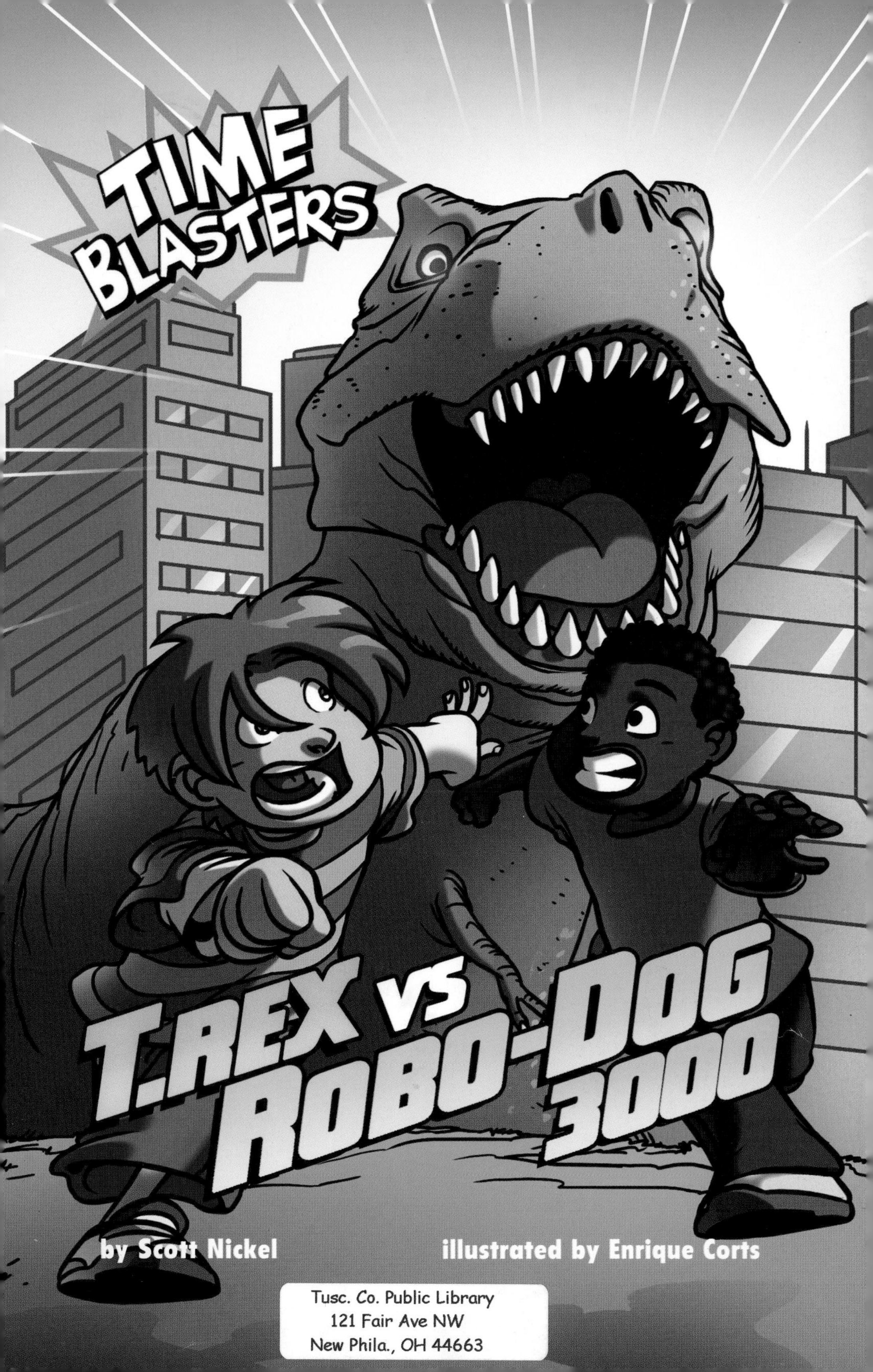
TIME BLASTERS
T.REX VS ROBO-DOG 3000
by Scott Nickel
illustrated by Enrique Corts

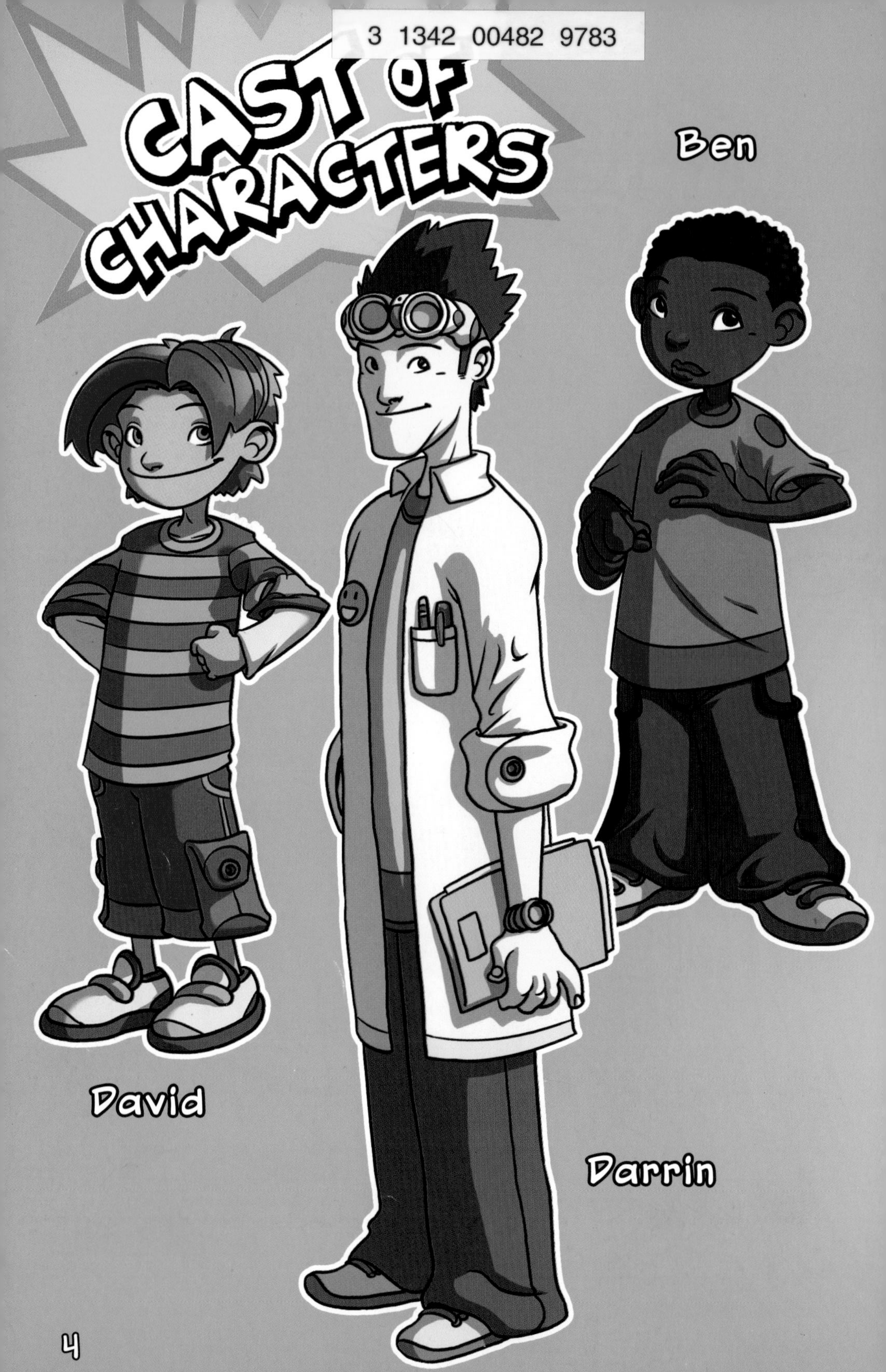
CAST OF CHARACTERS
Ben
David
Darrin

Brendan

Lisa

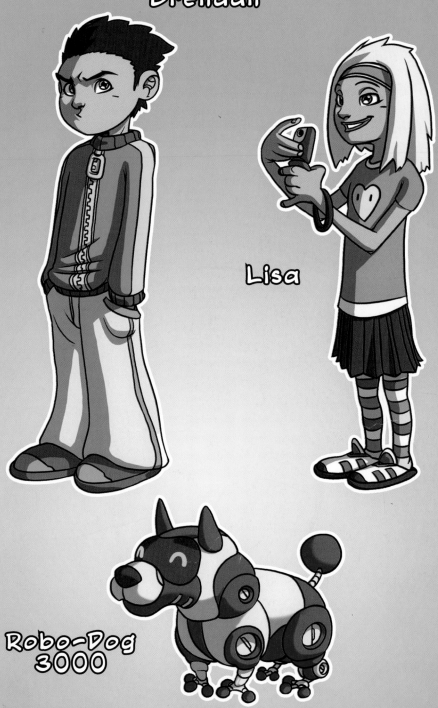

Robo-Dog 3000

One day in David's backyard . . .

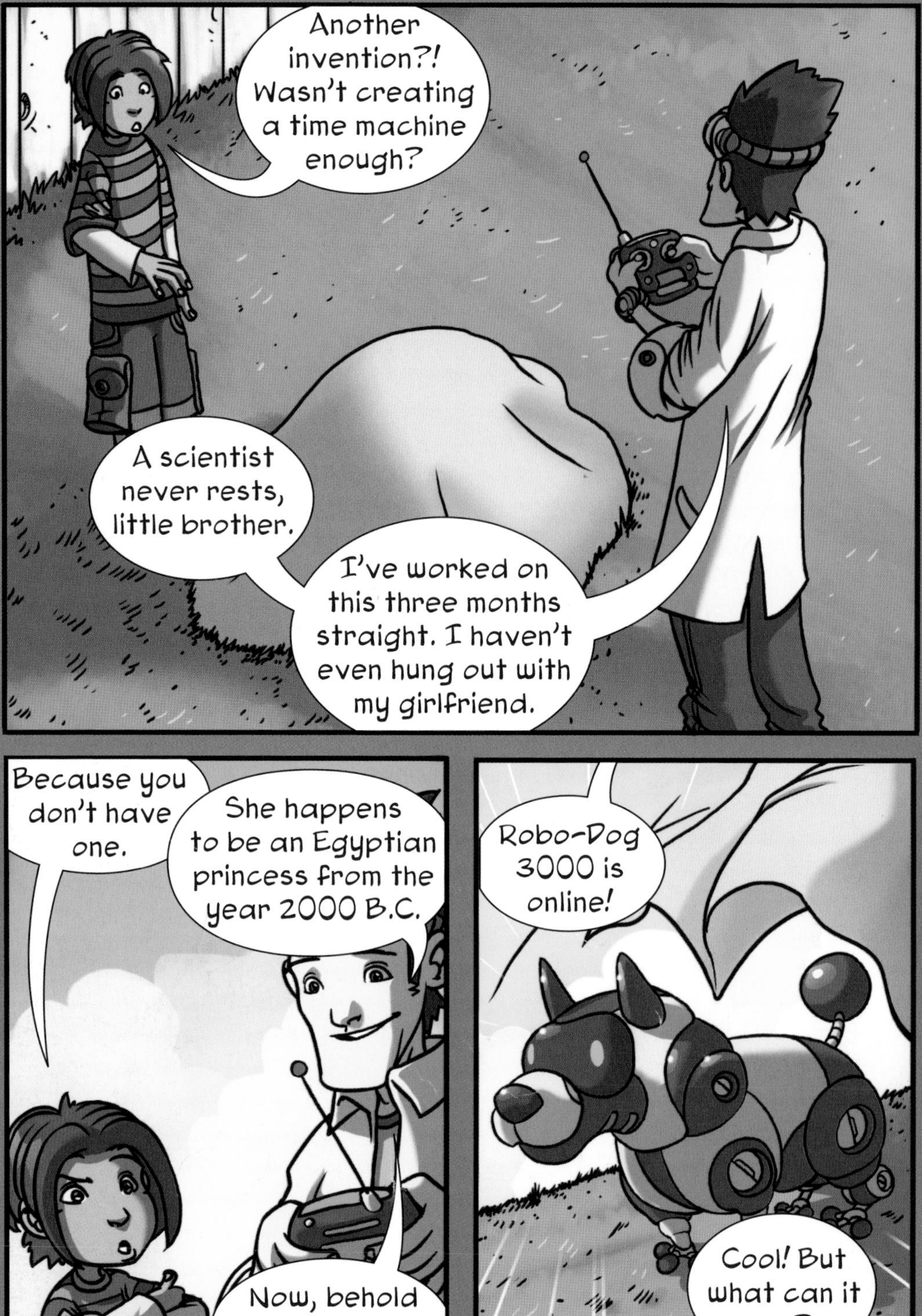
Another invention?! Wasn't creating a time machine enough?
A scientist never rests, little brother.
I've worked on this three months straight. I haven't even hung out with my girlfriend.
Because you don't have one.
She happens to be an Egyptian princess from the year 2000 B.C.
Now, behold the product of my genius!
Robo-Dog 3000 is online!
Cool! But what can it do?

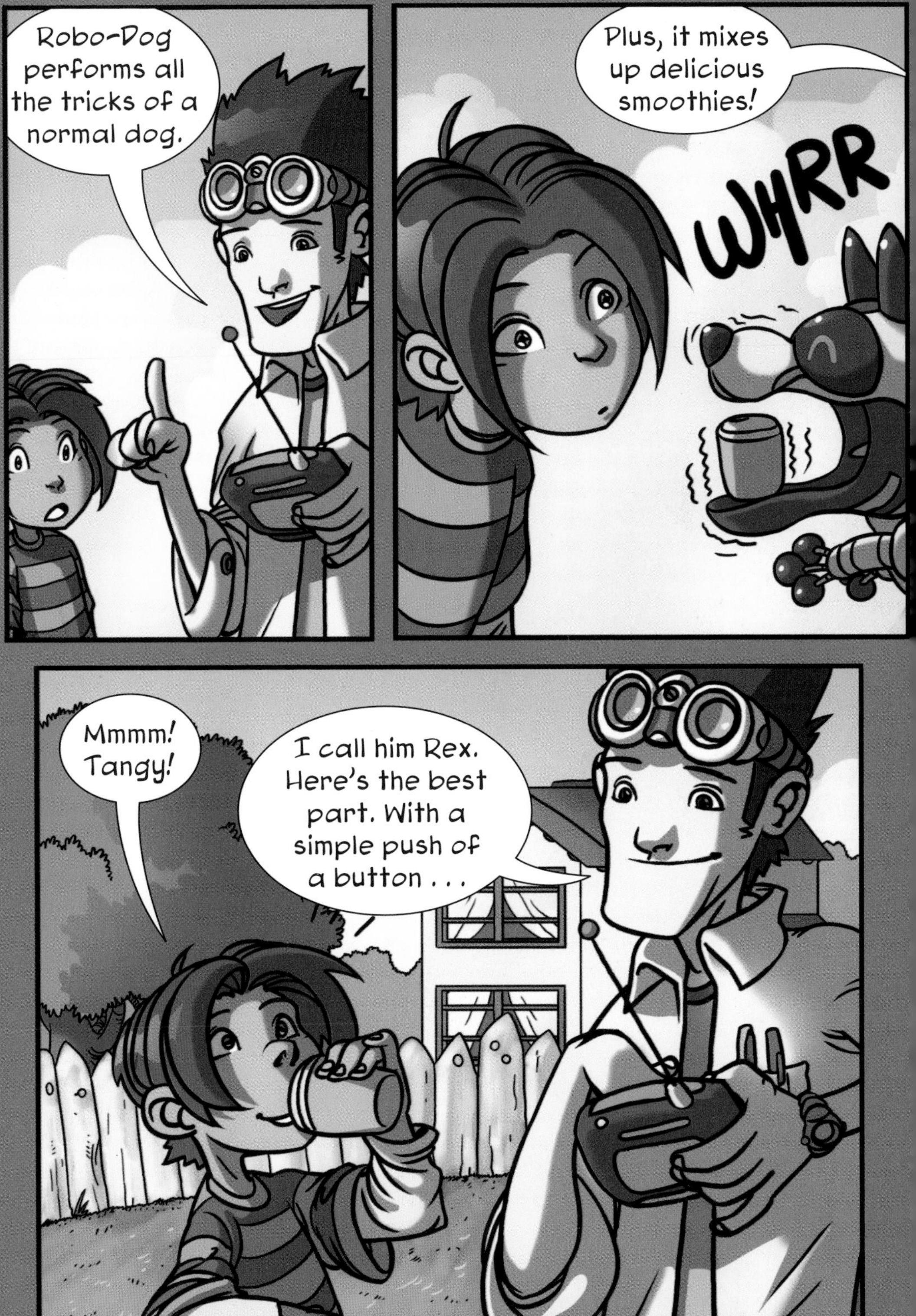
Robo-Dog performs all the tricks of a normal dog.
Plus, it mixes up delicious smoothies!
WHRR
Mmmm! Tangy!
I call him Rex. Here's the best part. With a simple push of a button . . .

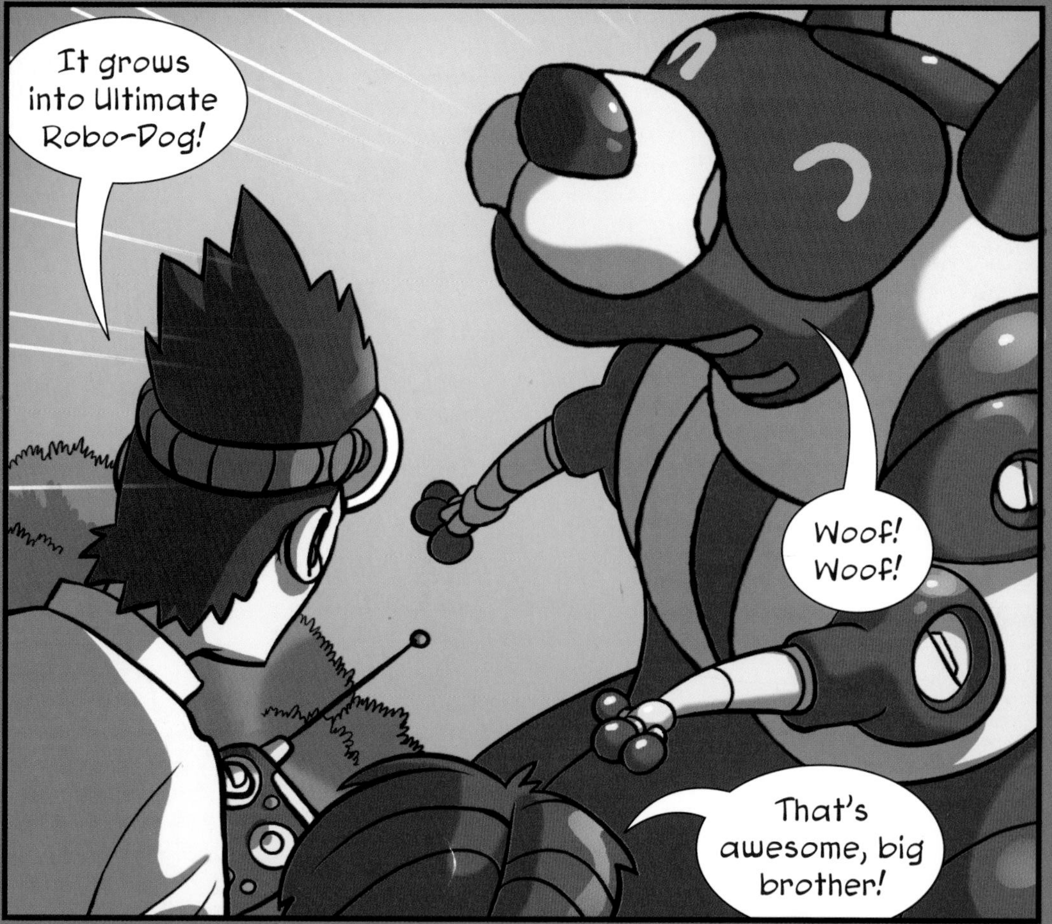
It grows into Ultimate Robo-Dog!
Woof! Woof!
That's awesome, big brother!

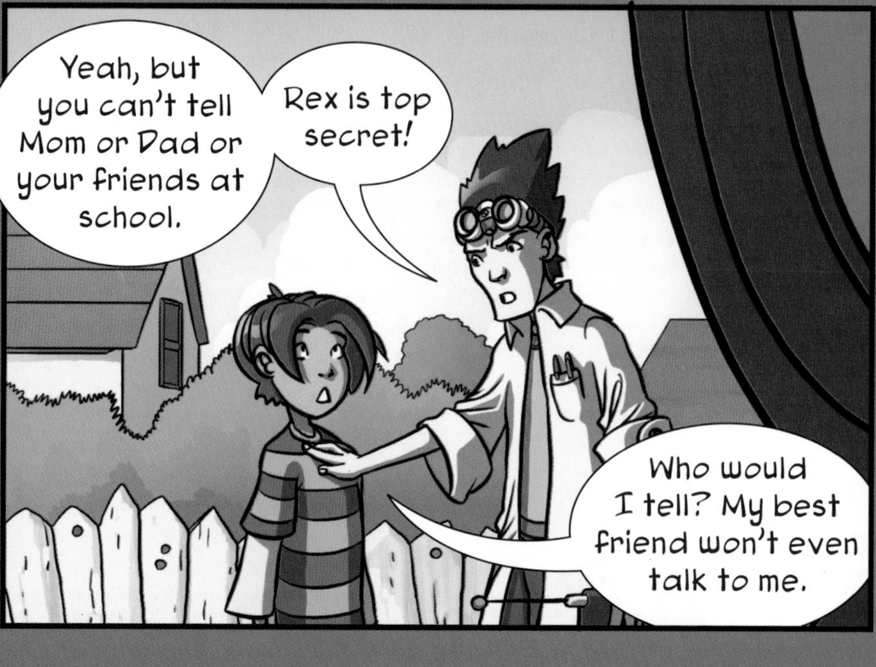
Yeah, but you can't tell Mom or Dad or your friends at school.
Rex is top secret!
Who would I tell? My best friend won't even talk to me.

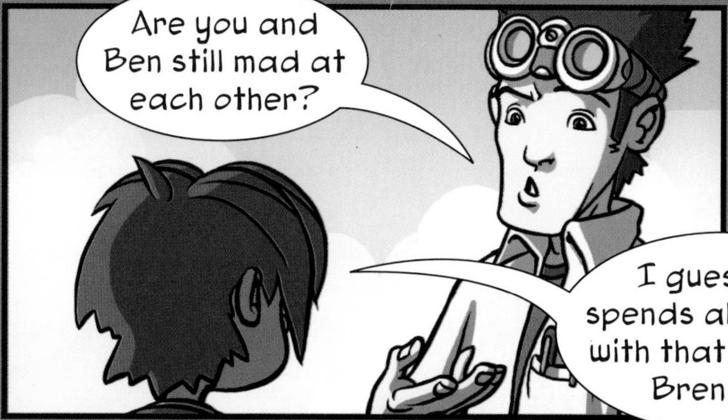
Are you and Ben still mad at each other?
I guess. He spends all his time with that new kid, Brendan.

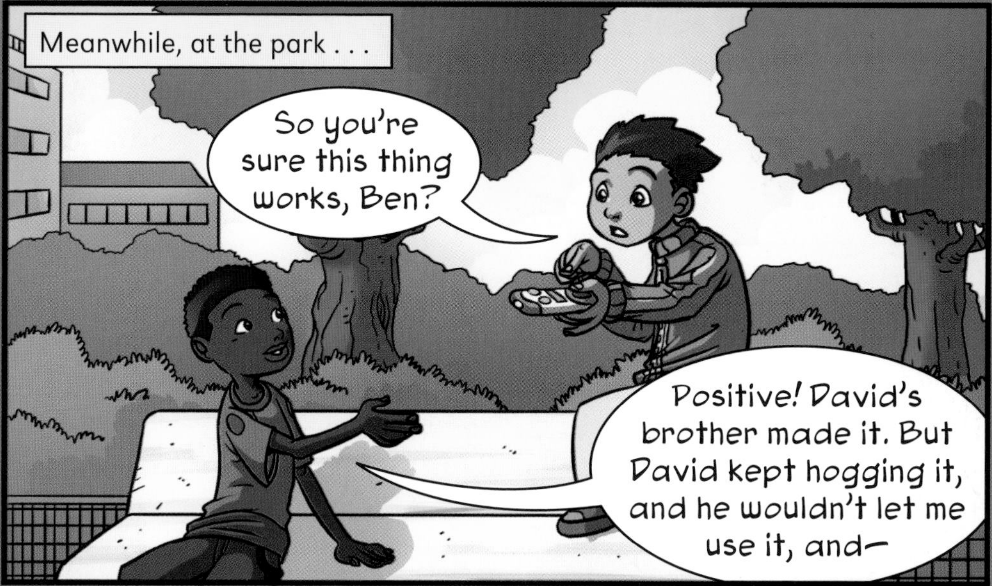
Meanwhile, at the park . . .
So you're sure this thing works, Ben?
Positive! David's brother made it. But David kept hogging it, and he wouldn't let me use it, and—

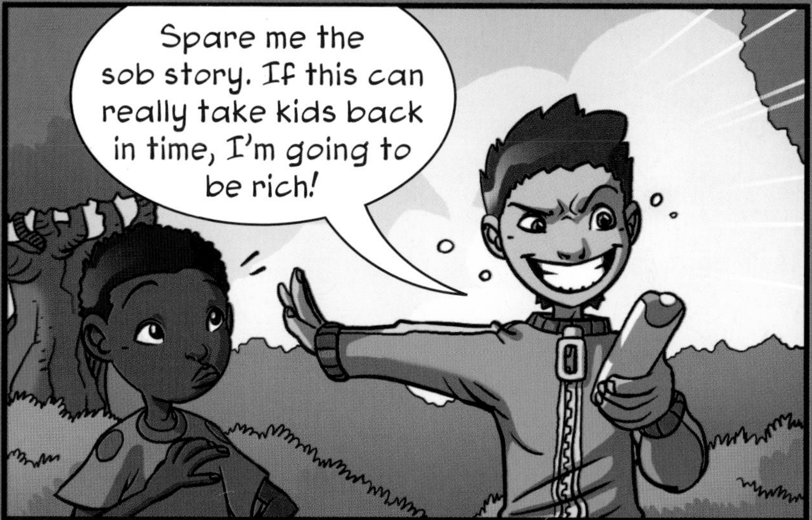
Spare me the sob story. If this can really take kids back in time, I'm going to be rich!

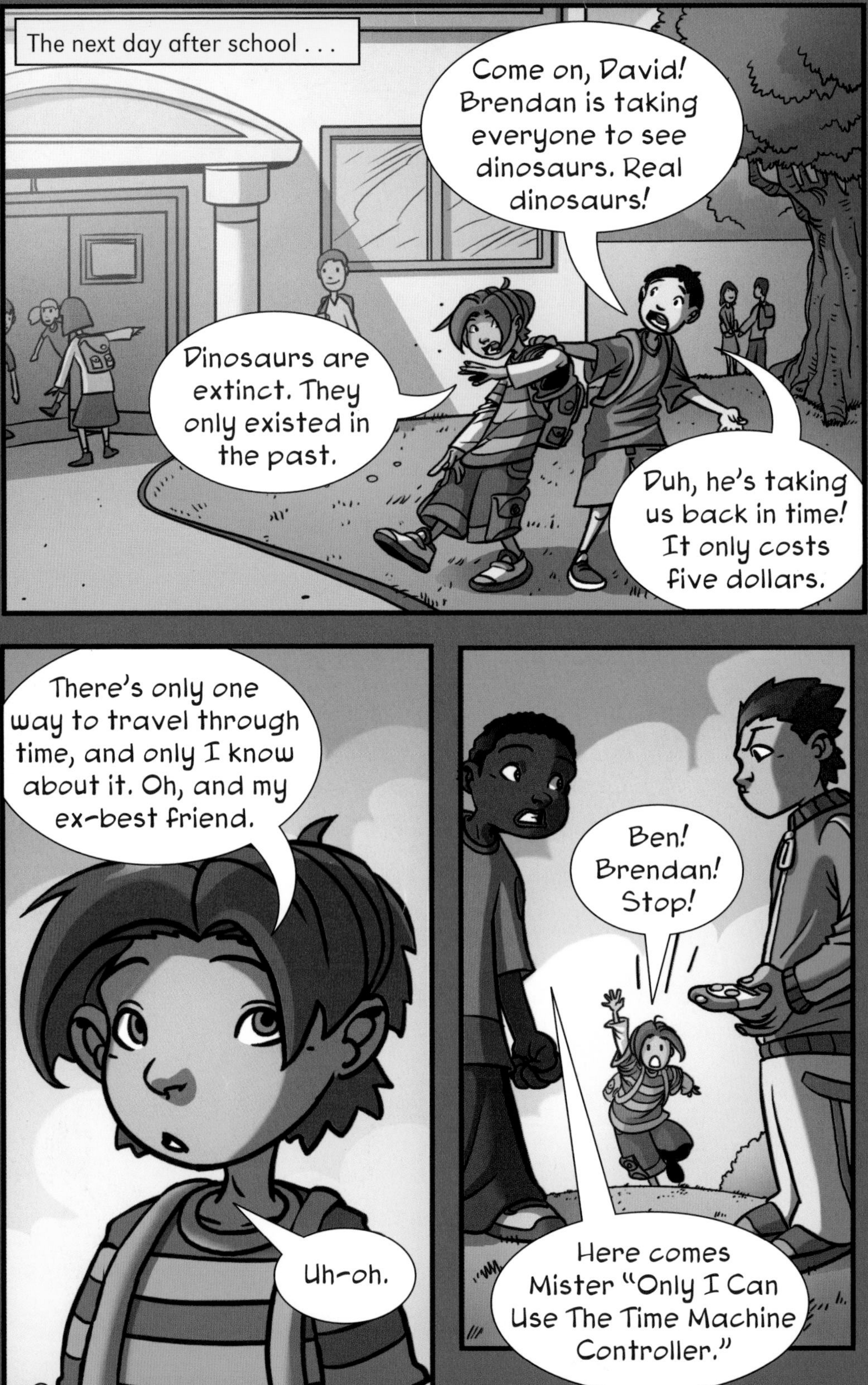
The next day after school . . .
Come on, David! Brendan is taking everyone to see dinosaurs. Real dinosaurs!
Dinosaurs are extinct. They only existed in the past.
Duh, he's taking us back in time! It only costs five dollars.
There's only one way to travel through time, and only I know about it. Oh, and my ex-best friend.
Uh-oh.
Ben! Brendan! Stop!
Here comes Mister "Only I Can Use The Time Machine Controller."

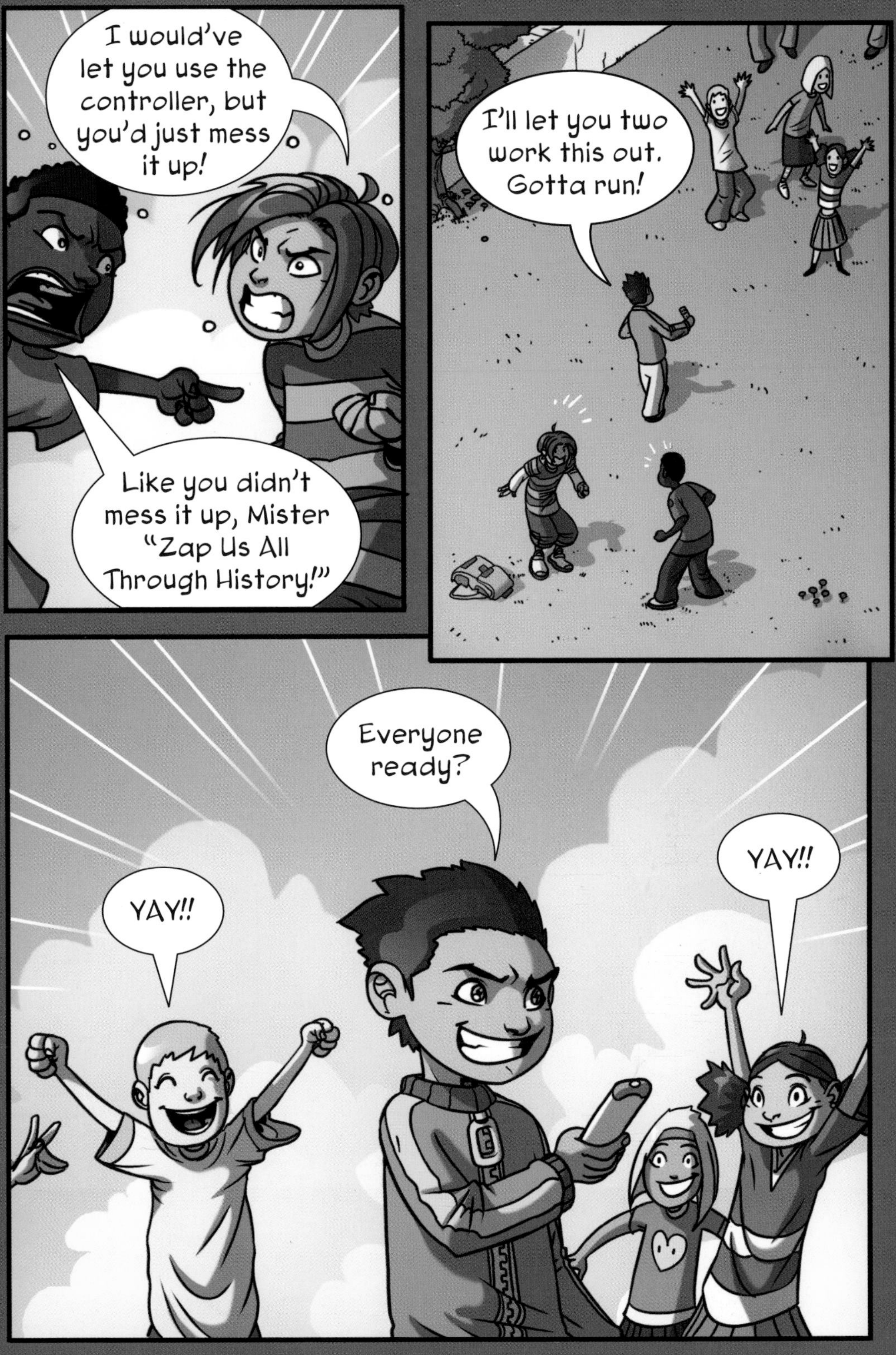
I would've let you use the controller, but you'd just mess it up!
Like you didn't mess it up, Mister "Zap Us All Through History!"
I'll let you two work this out. Gotta run!
Everyone ready?
YAY!!
YAY!!

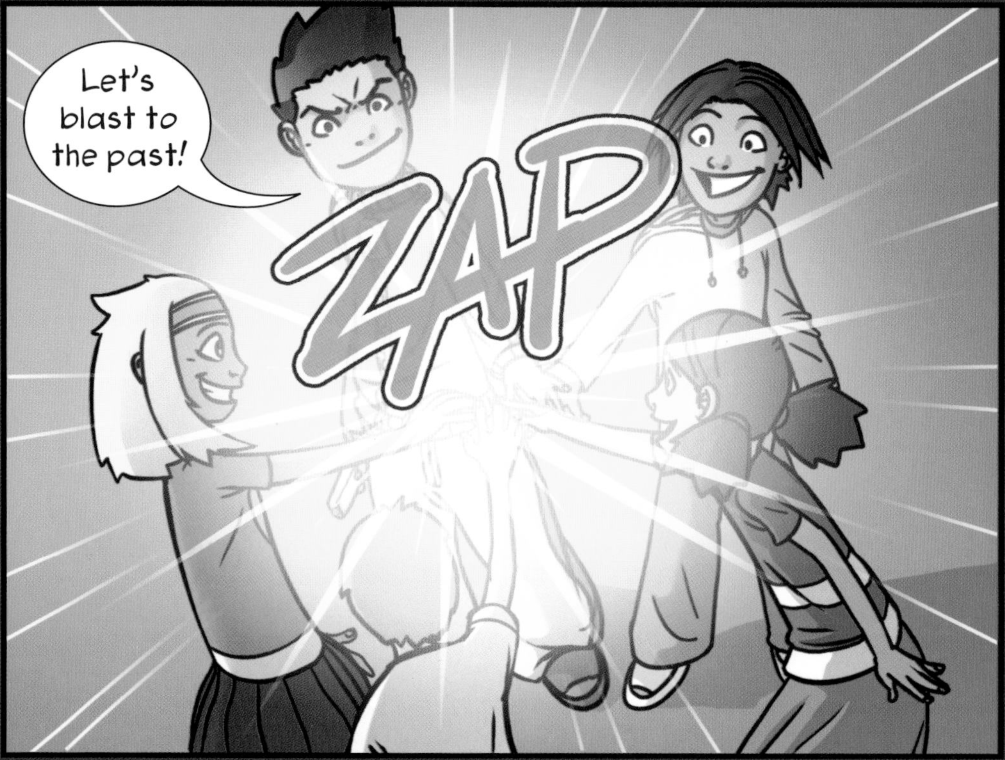
Let's blast to the past!
ZAP

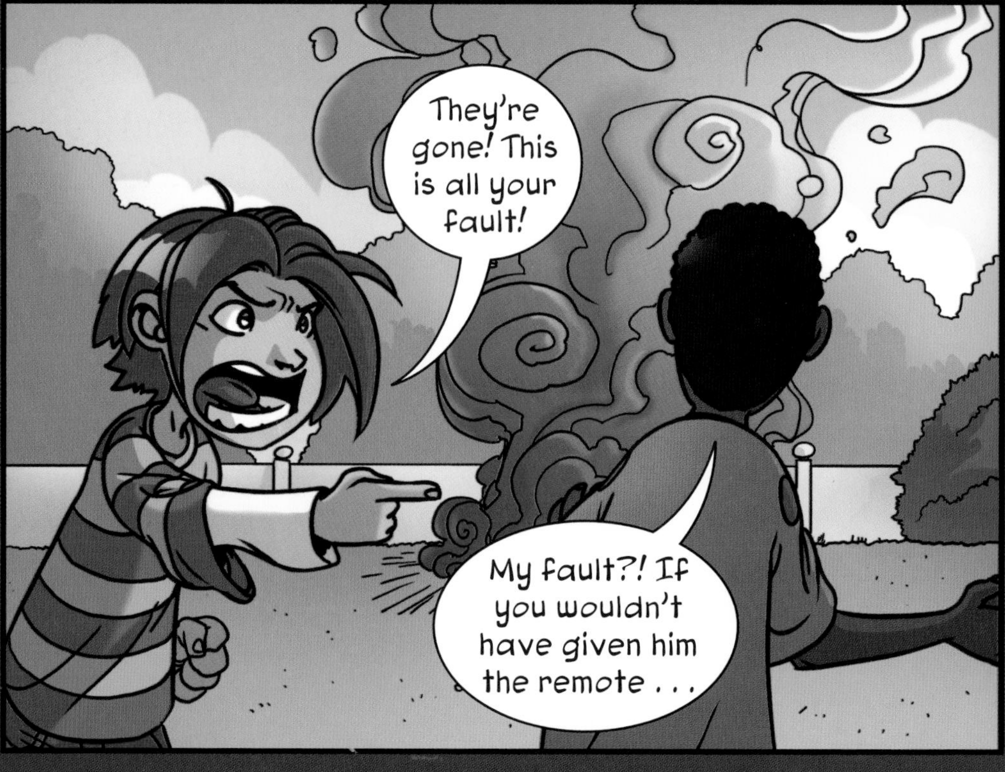
They're gone! This is all your fault!
My fault?! If you wouldn't have given him the remote . . .

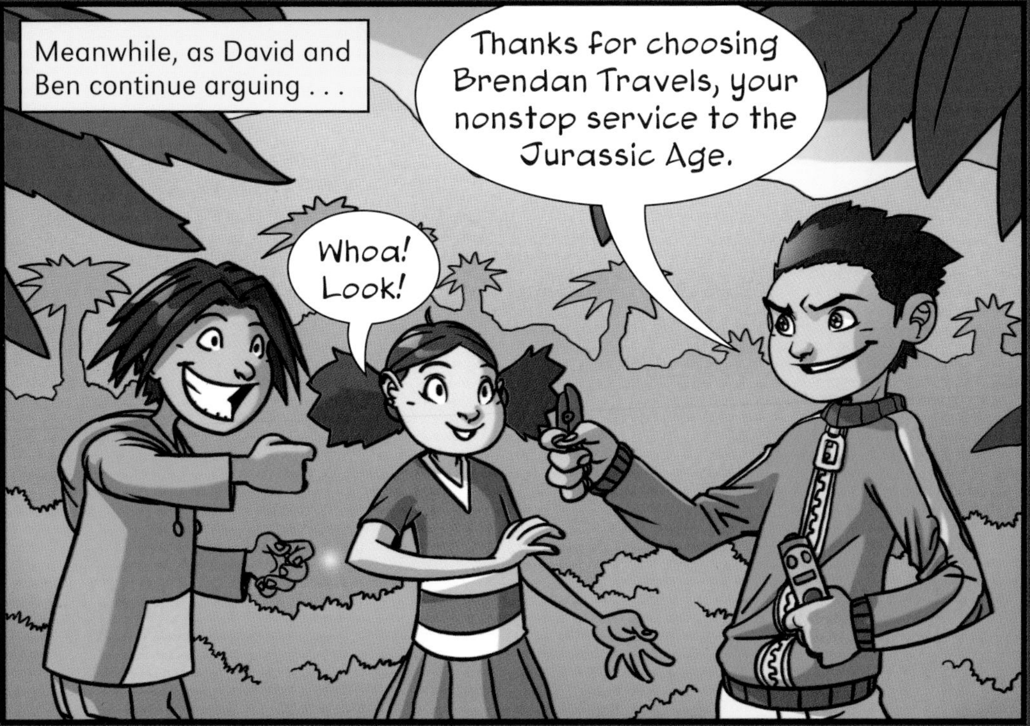
Meanwhile, as David and Ben continue arguing . . .
Thanks for choosing Brendan Travels, your nonstop service to the Jurassic Age.
Whoa! Look!

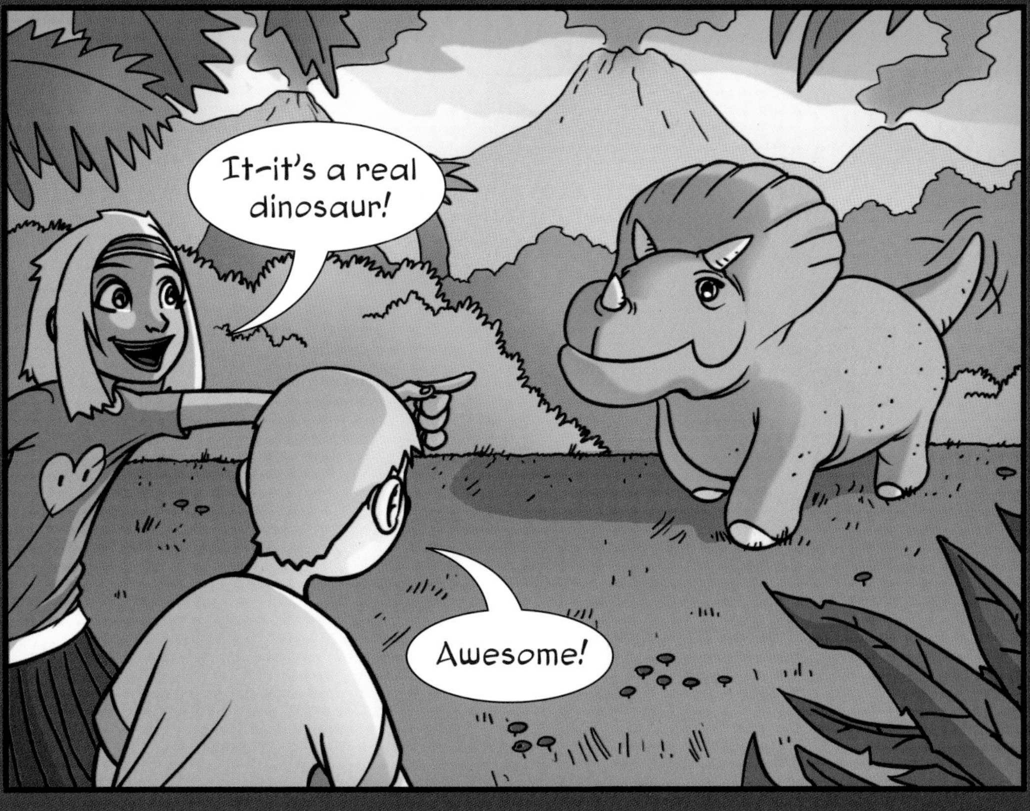
It-it's a real dinosaur!
Awesome!

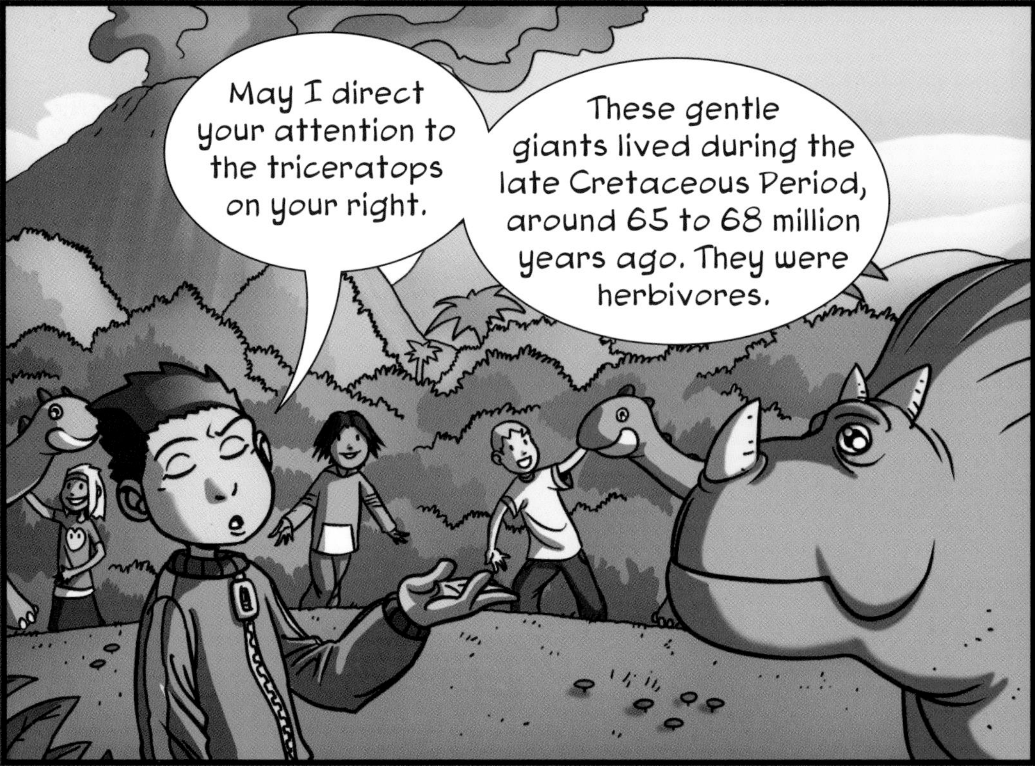
May I direct your attention to the triceratops on your right.
These gentle giants lived during the late Cretaceous Period, around 65 to 68 million years ago. They were herbivores.

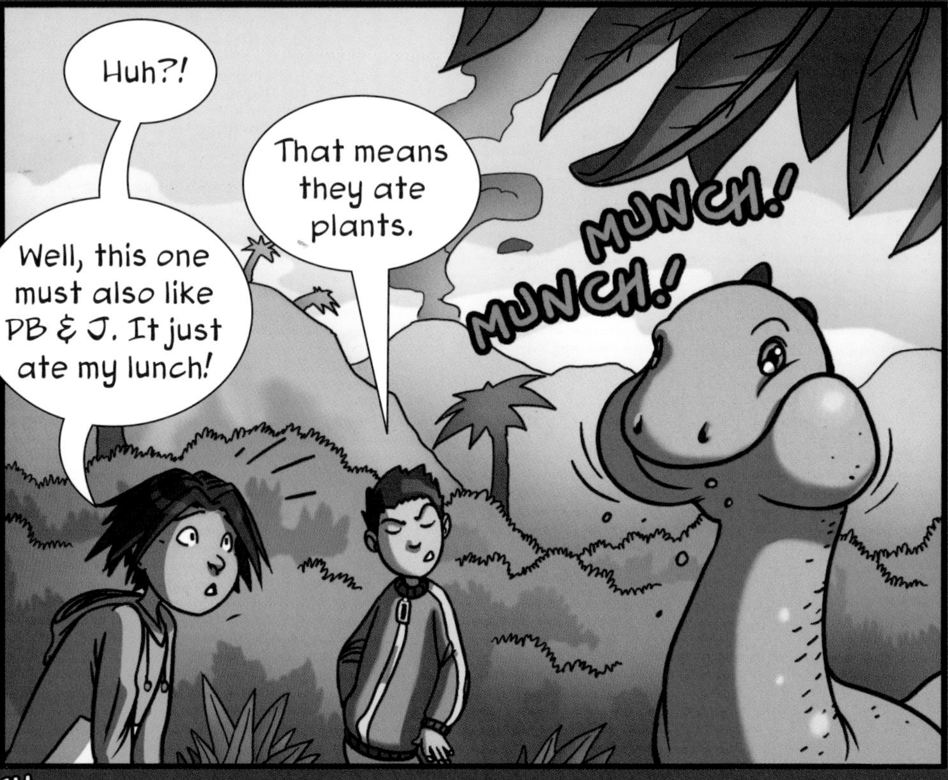
Huh?!
That means they ate plants.
Well, this one must also like PB & J. It just ate my lunch!
MUNCH!
MUNCH!

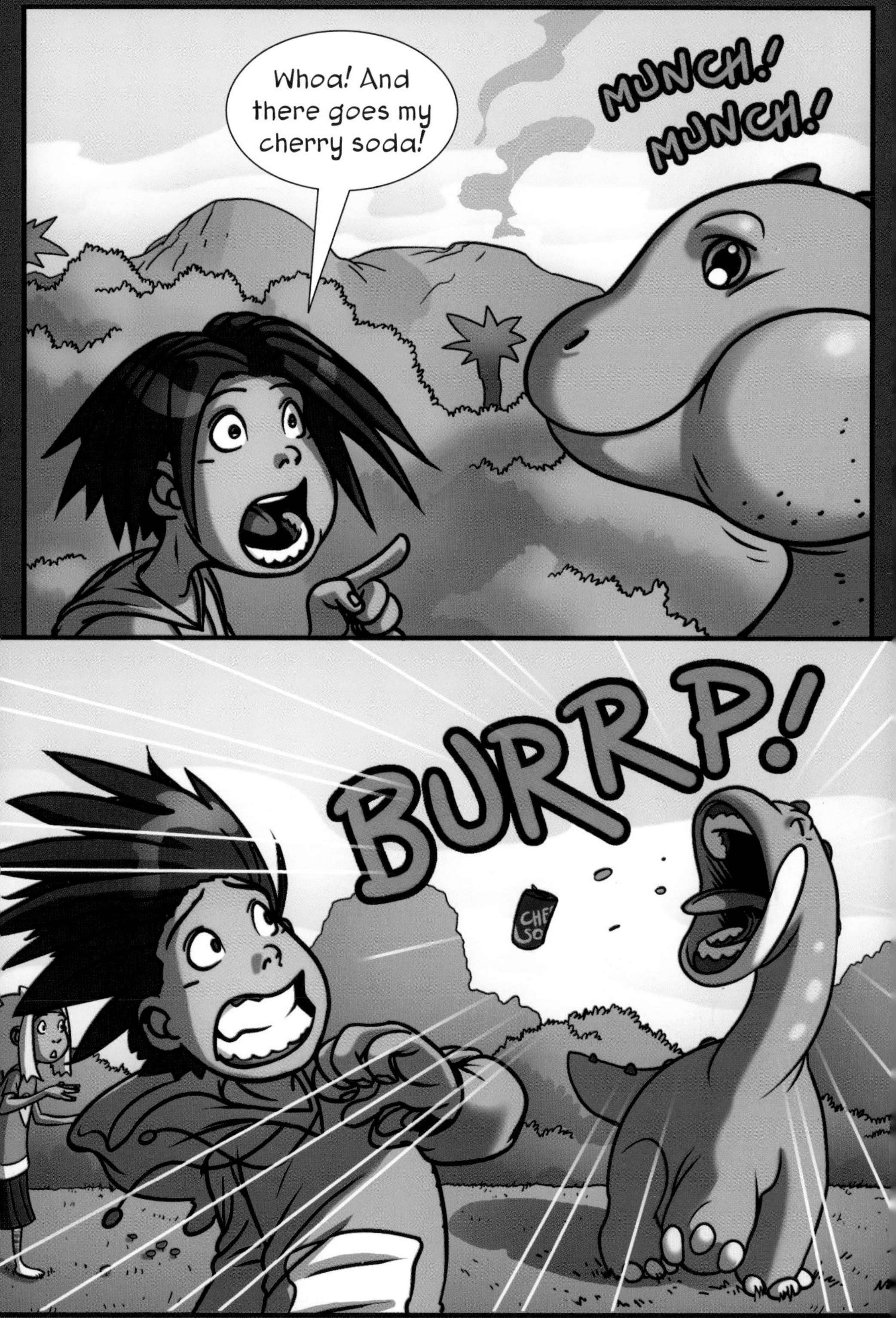
Whoa! And there goes my cherry soda!
MUNCH! MUNCH!
BURRP!

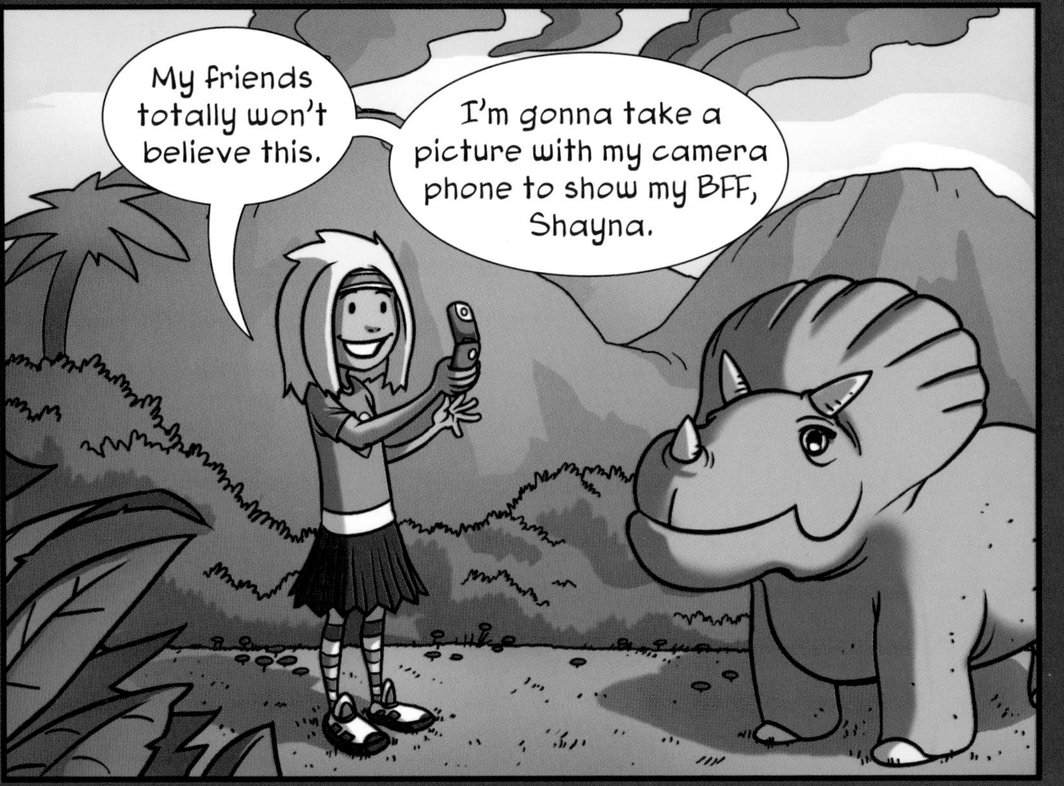
My friends totally won't believe this.
I'm gonna take a picture with my camera phone to show my BFF, Shayna.

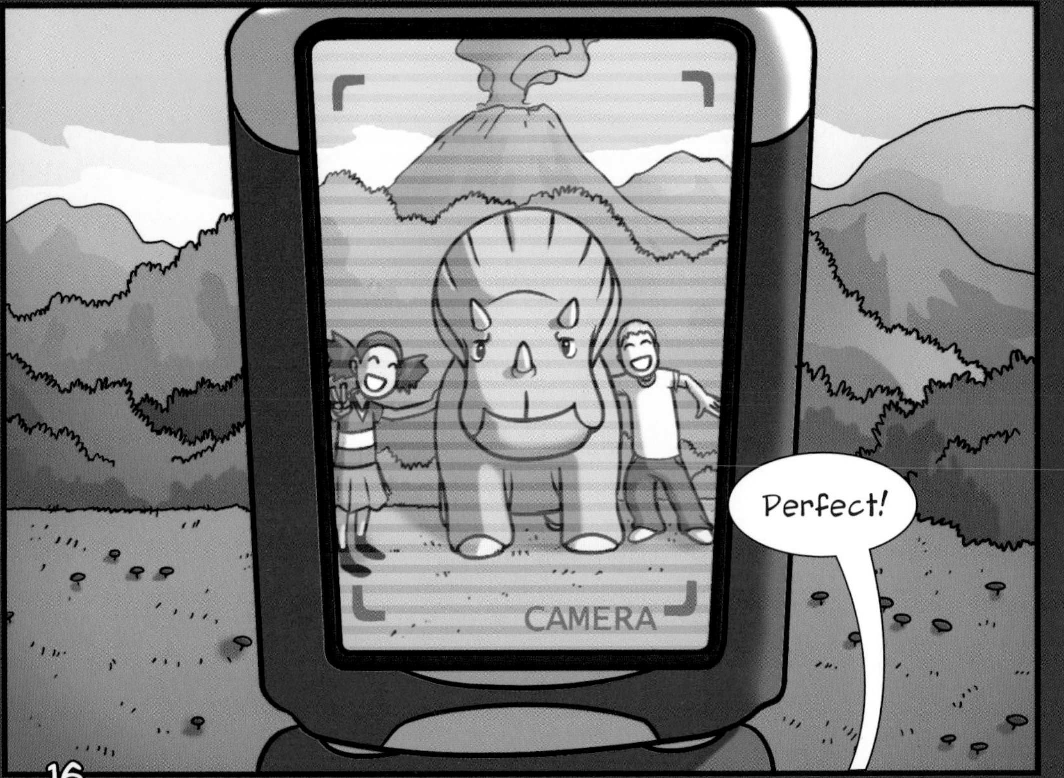
CAMERA
Perfect!

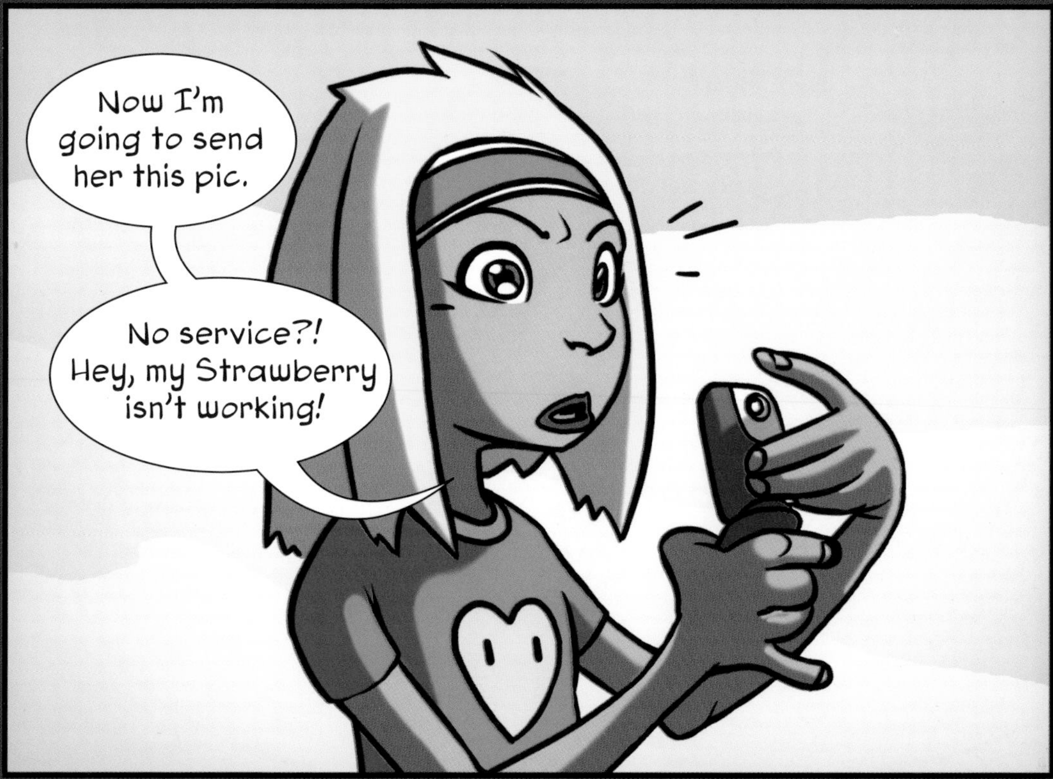
Now I'm going to send her this pic.
No service?! Hey, my Strawberry isn't working!

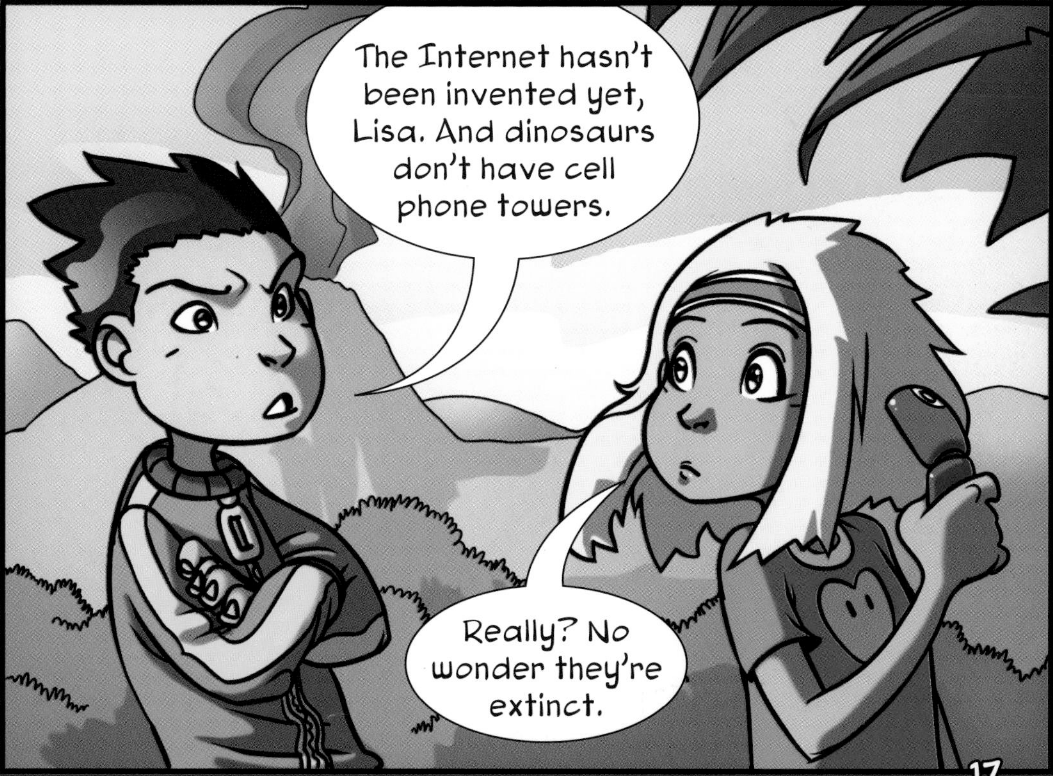
The Internet hasn't been invented yet, Lisa. And dinosaurs don't have cell phone towers.
Really? No wonder they're extinct.

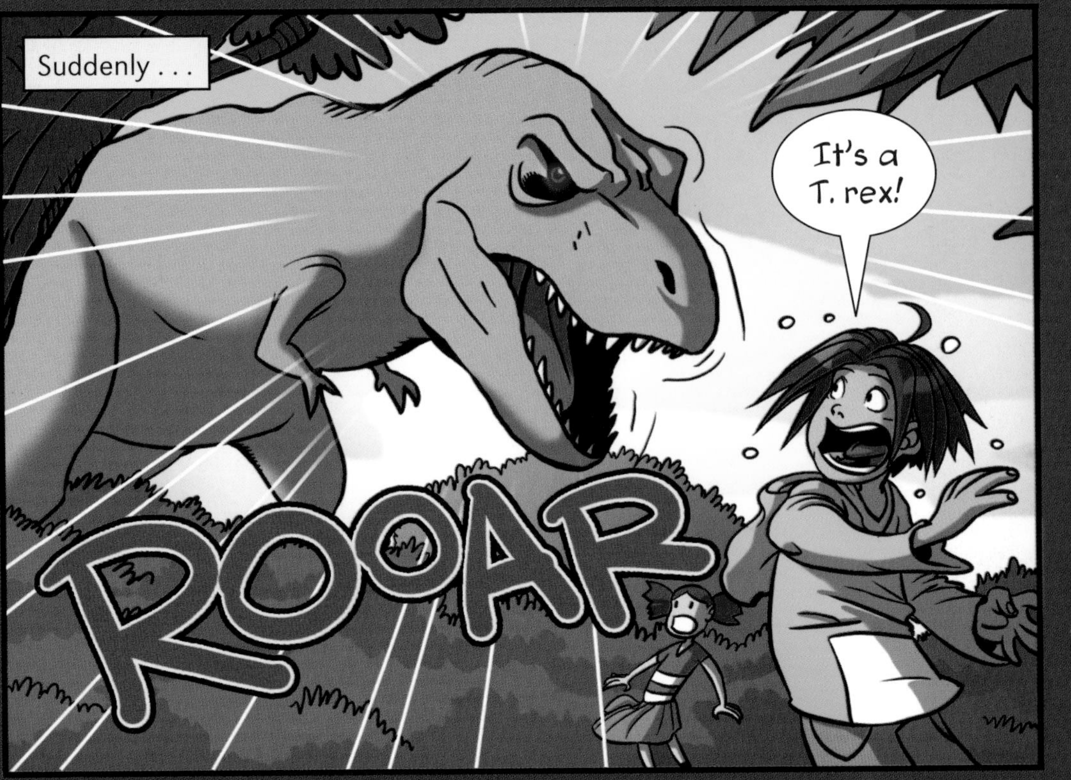
Suddenly . . .
It's a T. rex!
ROOAR

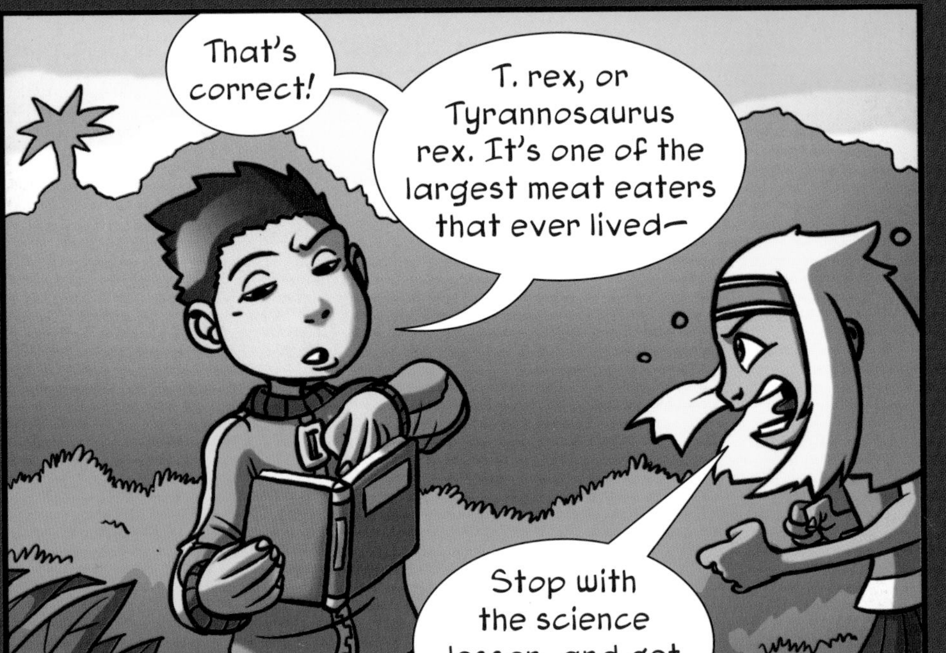
That's correct!
T. rex, or Tyrannosaurus rex. It's one of the largest meat eaters that ever lived—
Stop with the science lesson, and get us out of here!

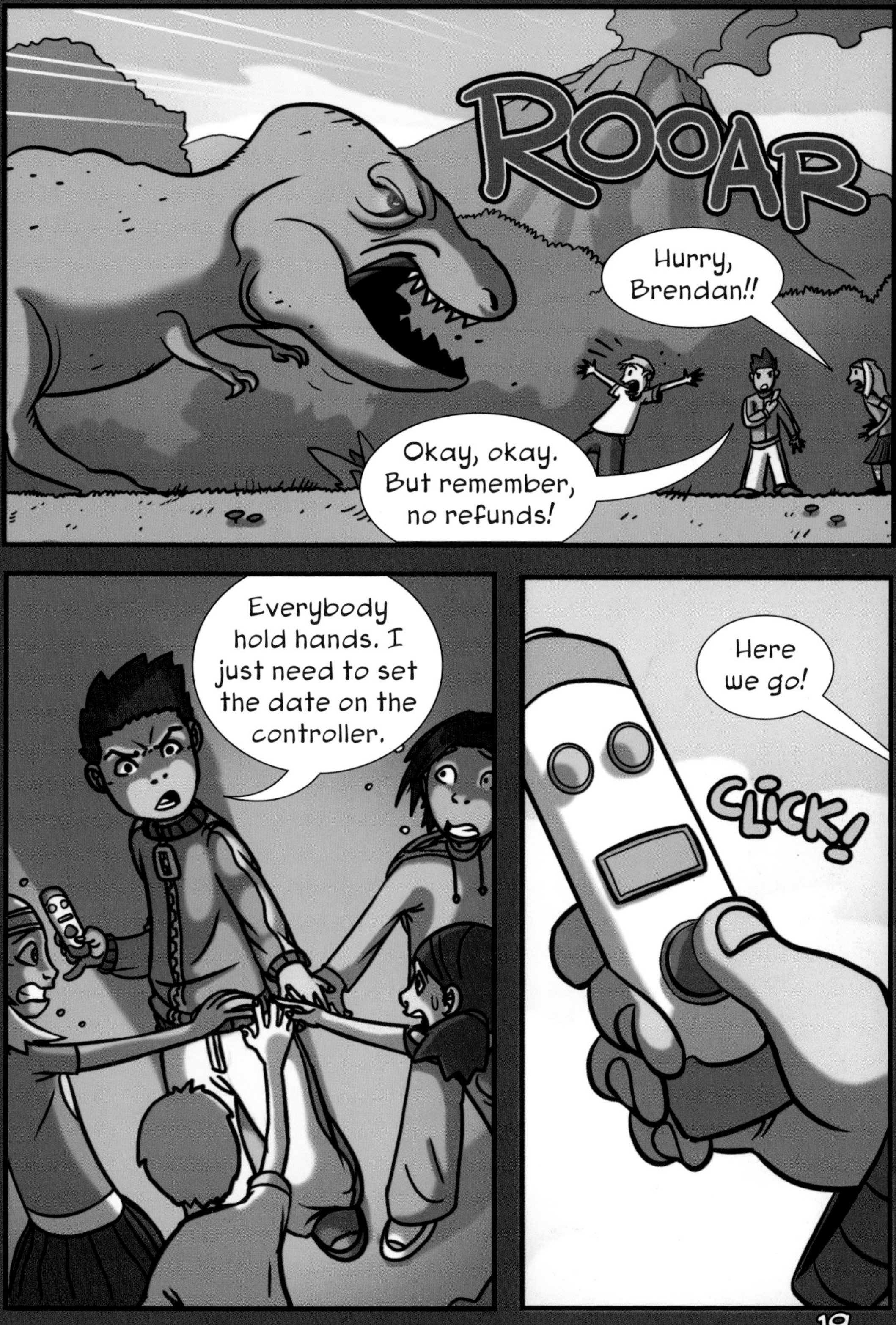
ROOAR
Hurry, Brendan!!
Okay, okay. But remember, no refunds!
Everybody hold hands. I just need to set the date on the controller.
Here we go!
CLICK!

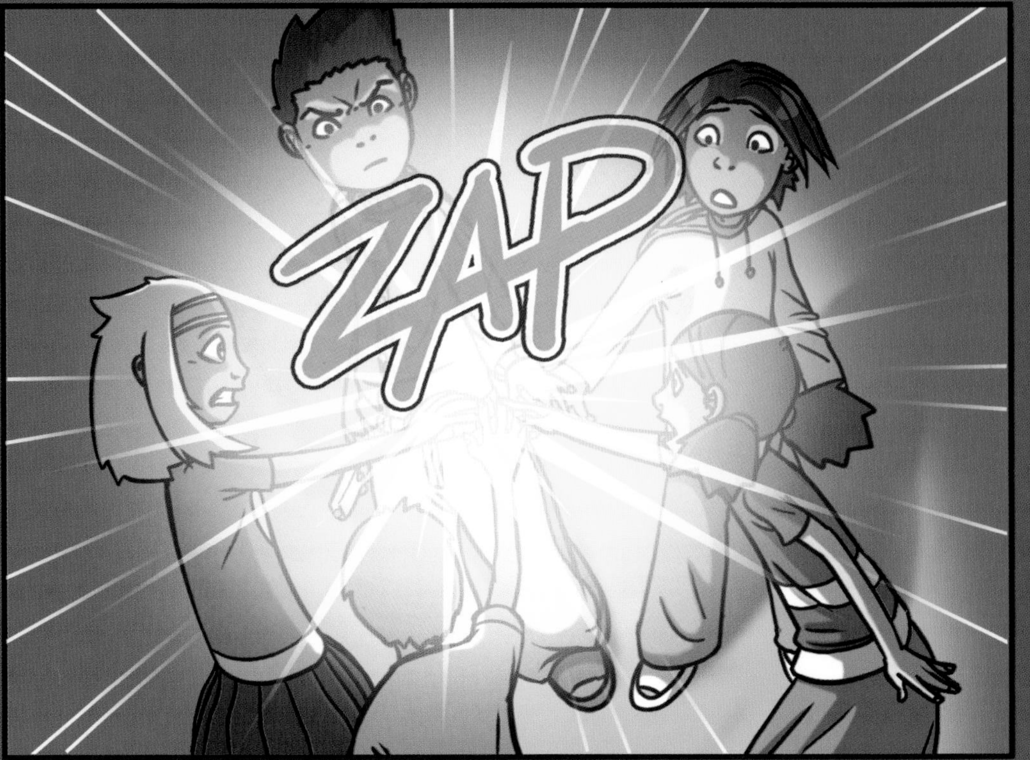
ZAP

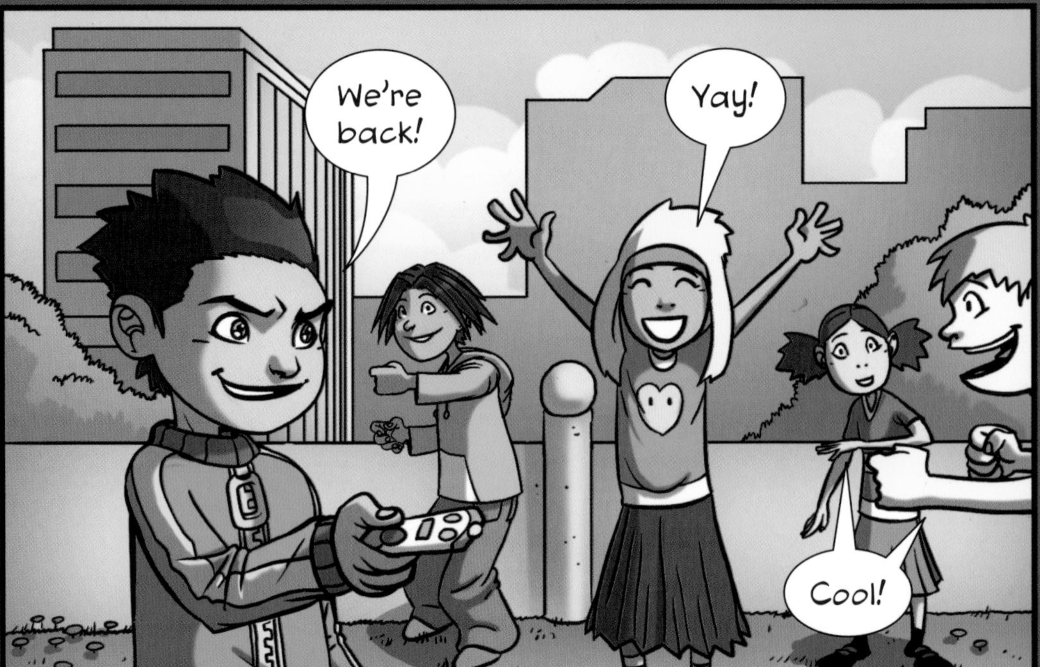
We're back!
Yay!
Cool!

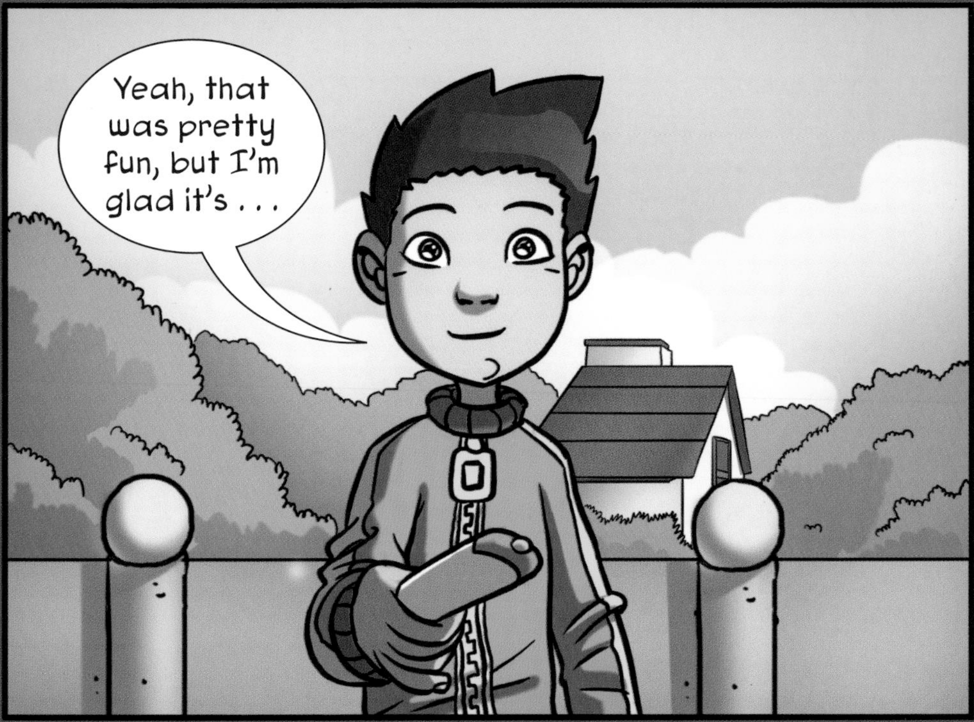
Yeah, that was pretty fun, but I'm glad it's . . .

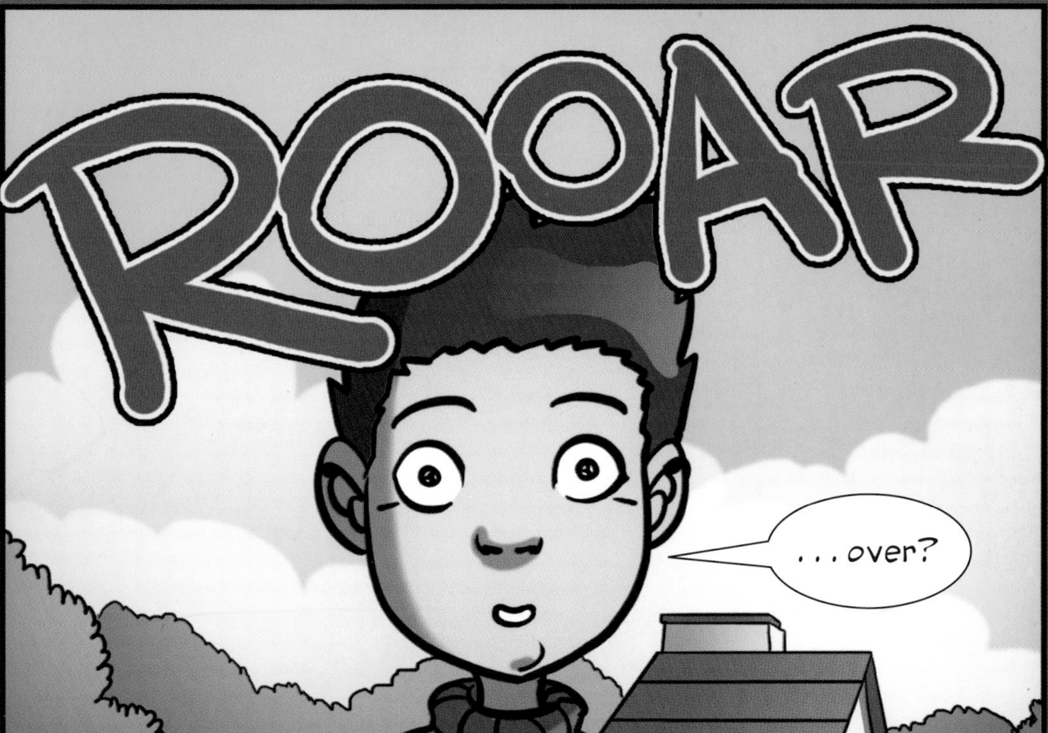
ROOAR
. . . over?

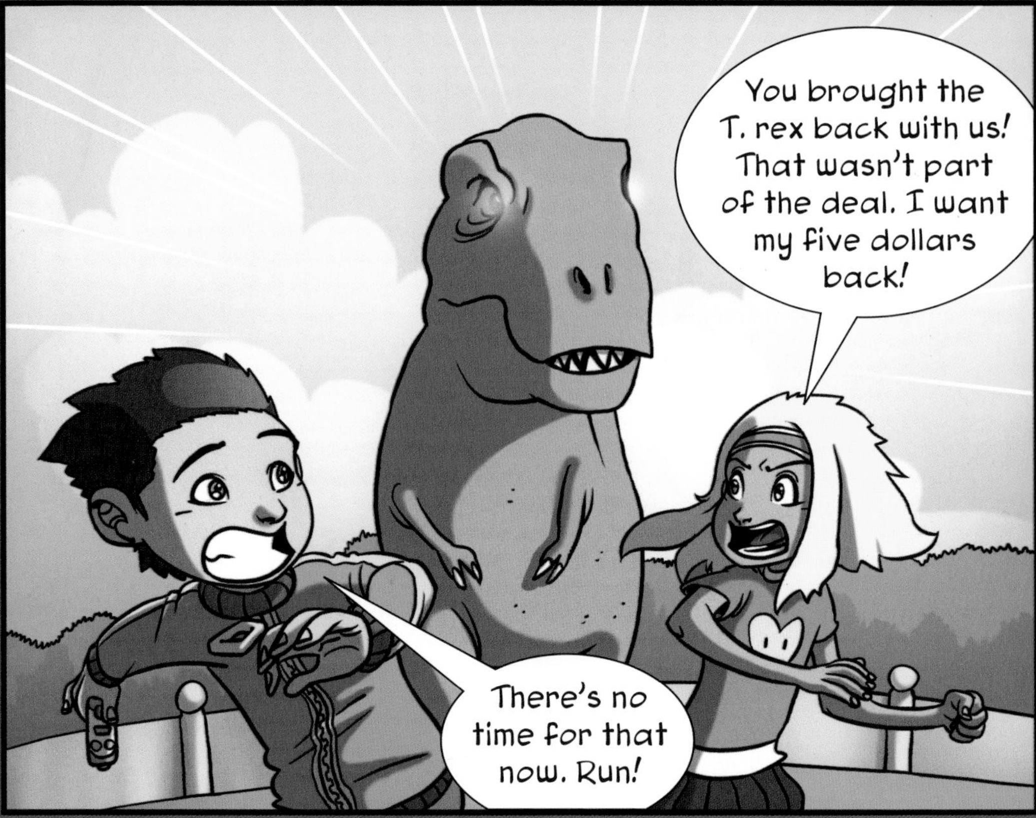
You brought the T. rex back with us! That wasn't part of the deal. I want my five dollars back!
There's no time for that now. Run!

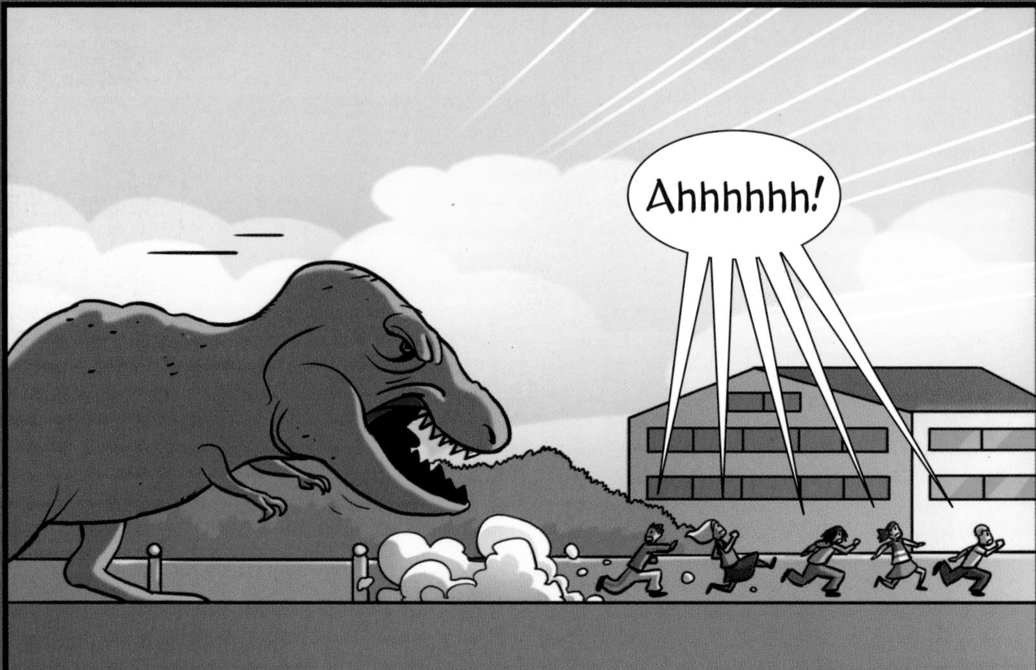
Ahhhhhh!

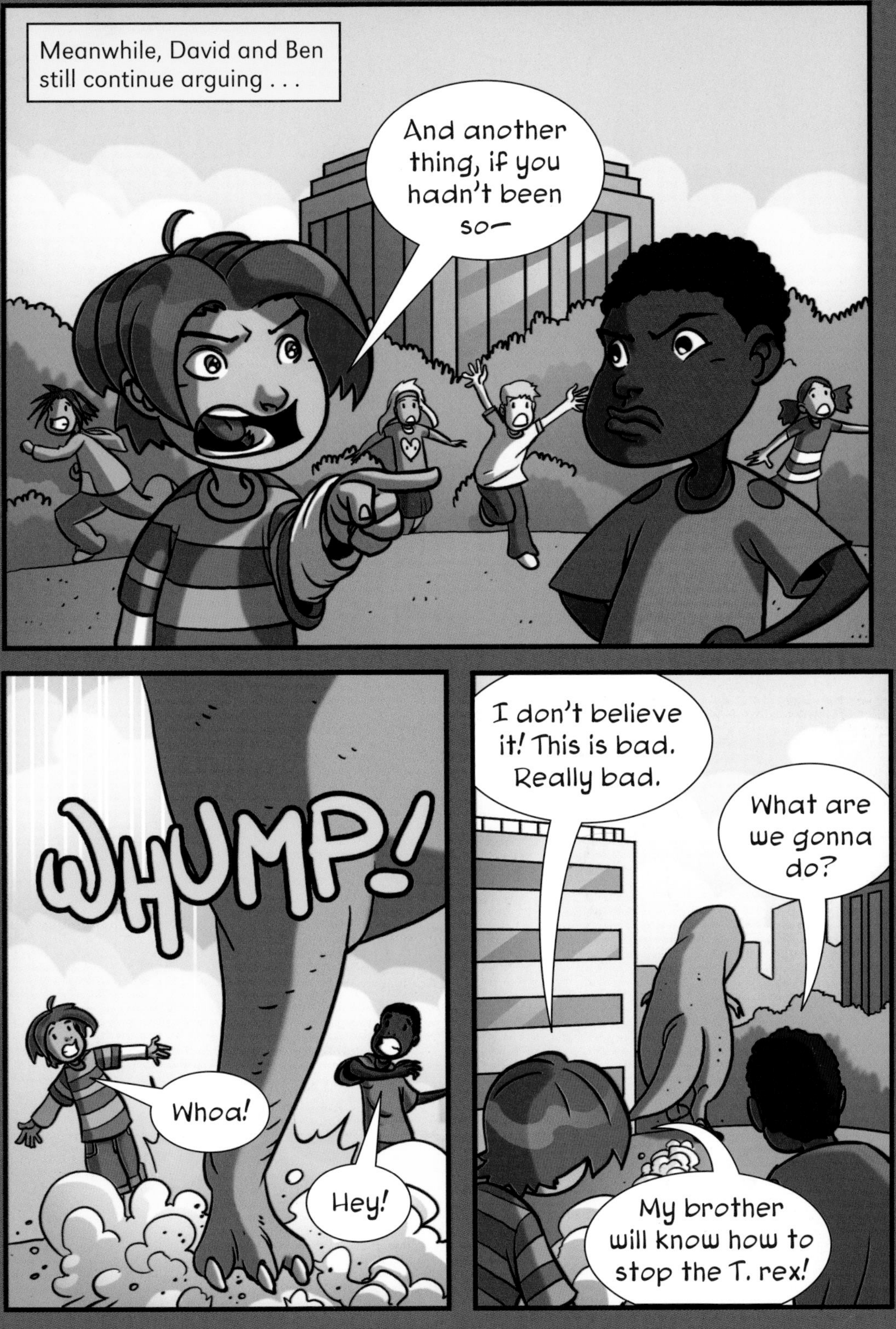

Meanwhile, David and Ben still continue arguing . . .
And another thing, if you hadn't been so—
WHUMP!
Whoa!
Hey!
I don't believe it! This is bad. Really bad.
What are we gonna do?
My brother will know how to stop the T. rex!

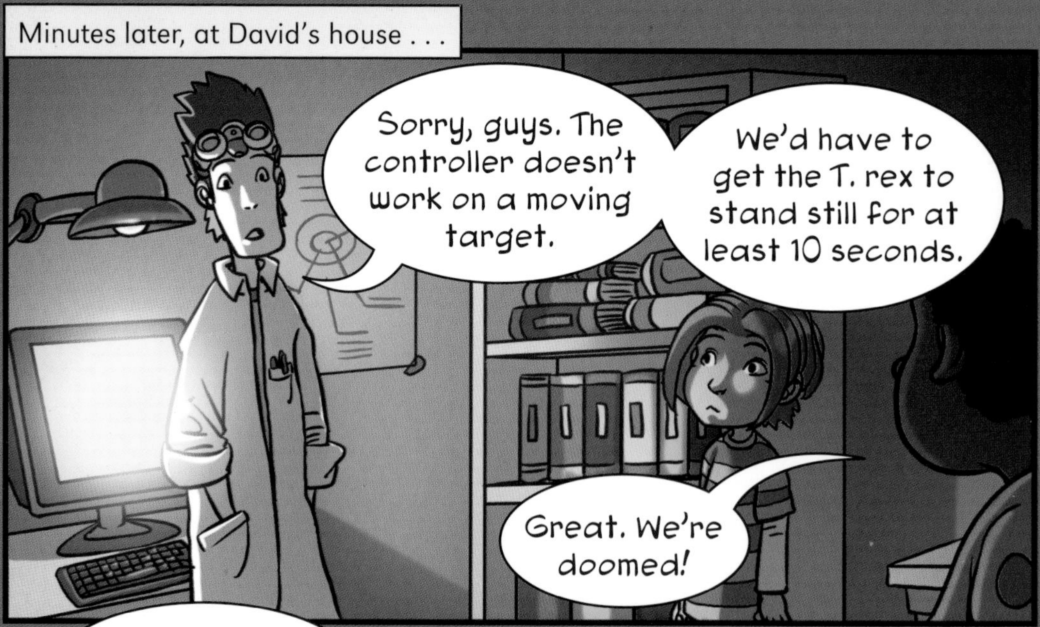
Minutes later, at David's house . . .
Sorry, guys. The controller doesn't work on a moving target.
We'd have to get the T. rex to stand still for at least 10 seconds.
Great. We're doomed!

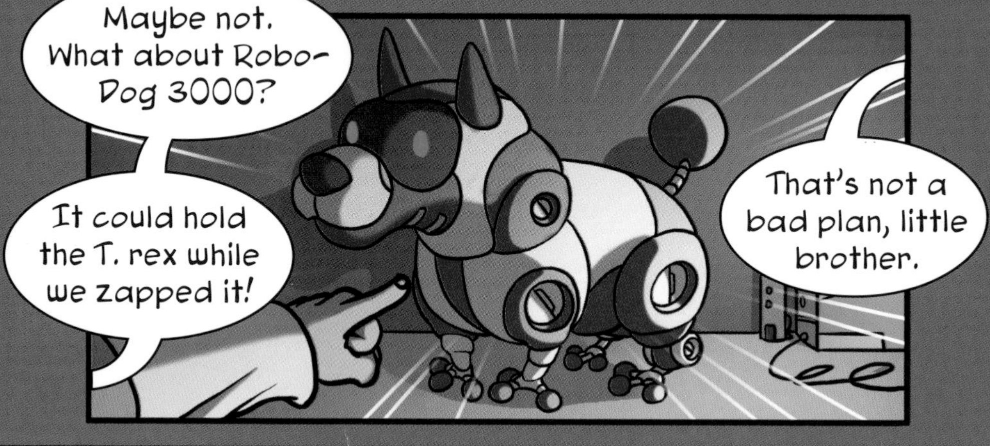
Maybe not. What about Robo-Dog 3000?
It could hold the T. rex while we zapped it!
That's not a bad plan, little brother.

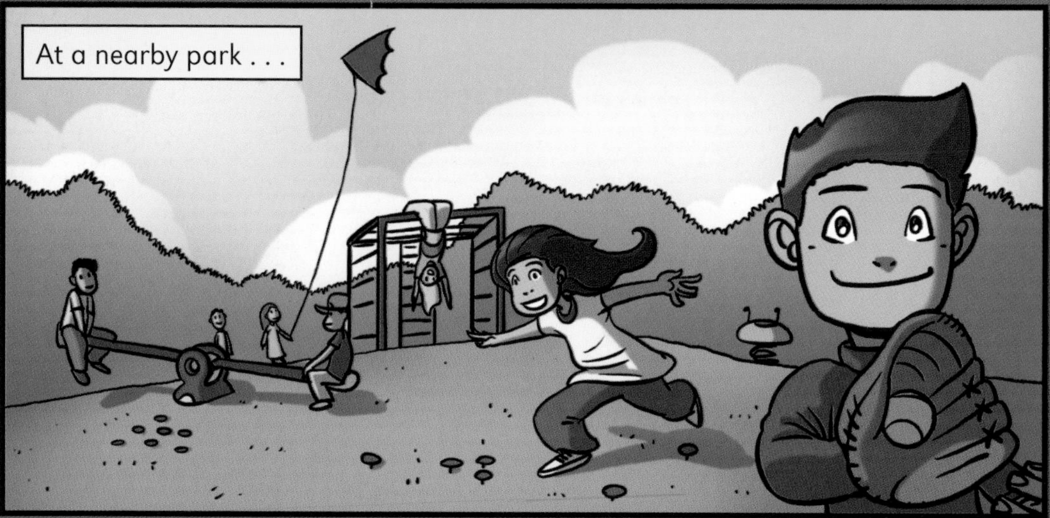
At a nearby park . . .

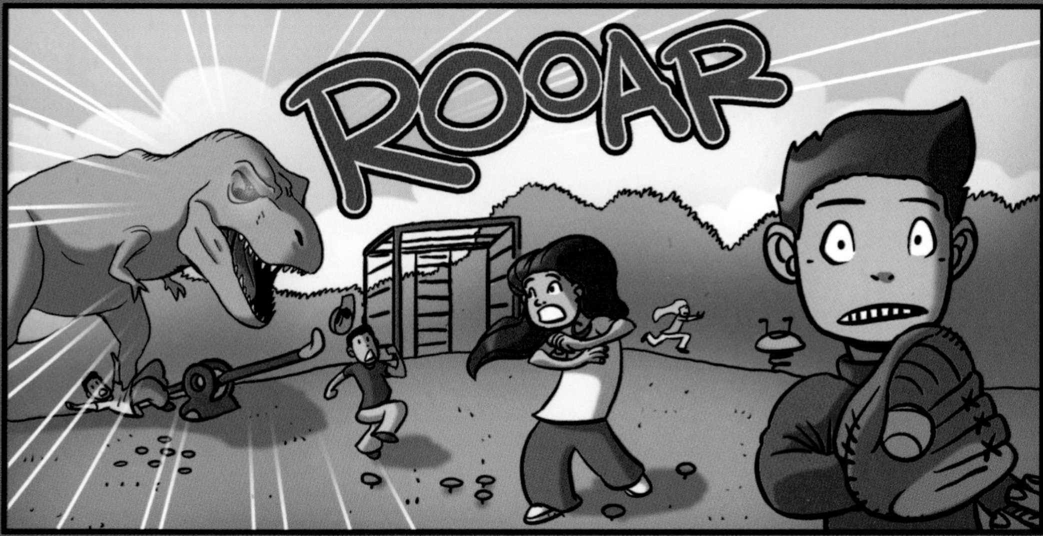
ROOAR

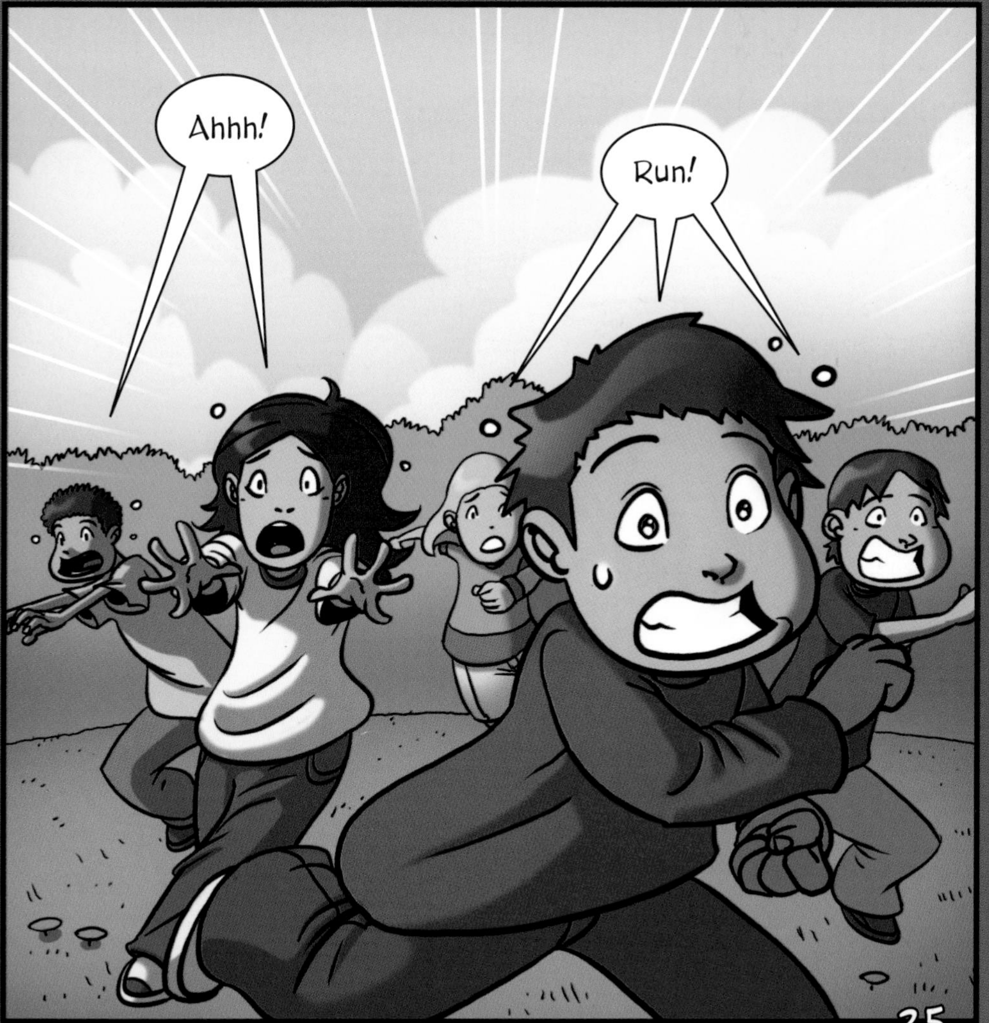
Ahhh!
Run!

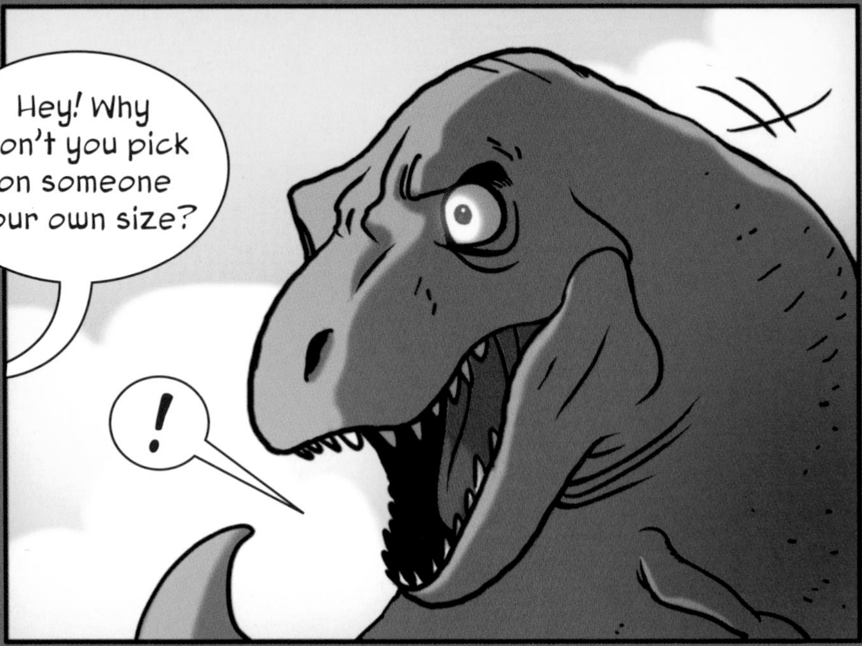
Hey! Why don't you pick on someone your own size?
!

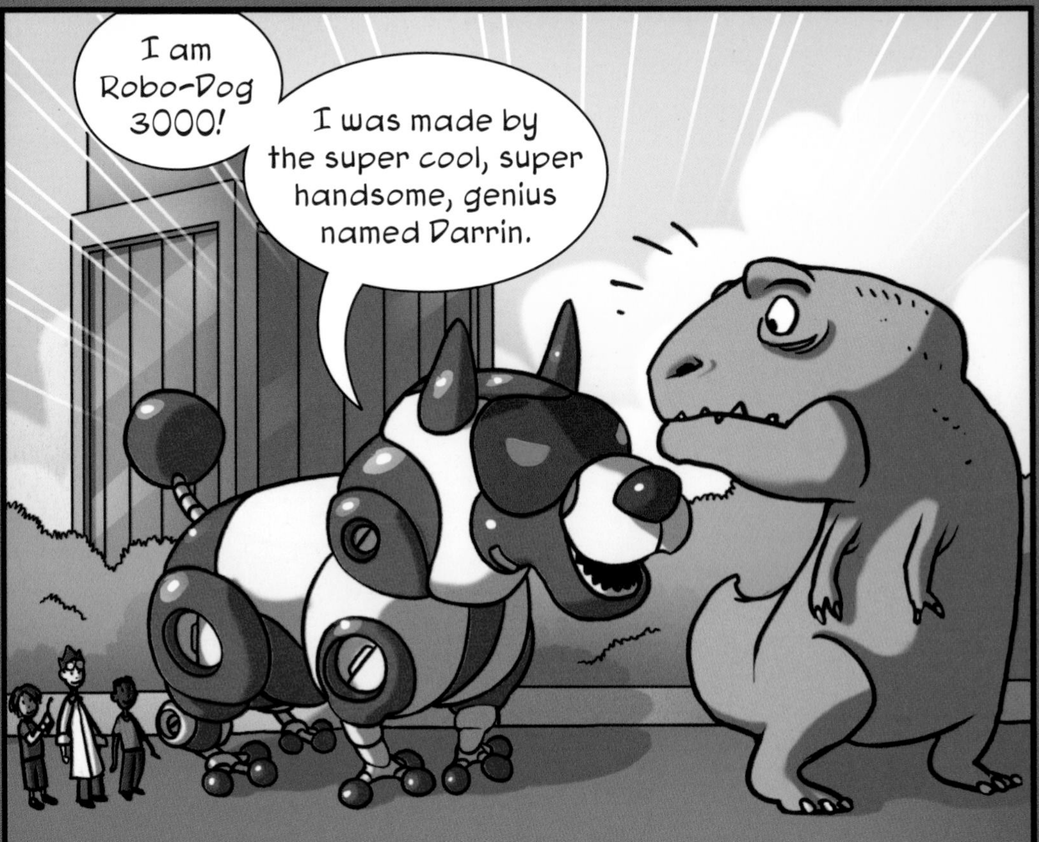
I am Robo-Dog 3000!
I was made by the super cool, super handsome, genius named Darrin.

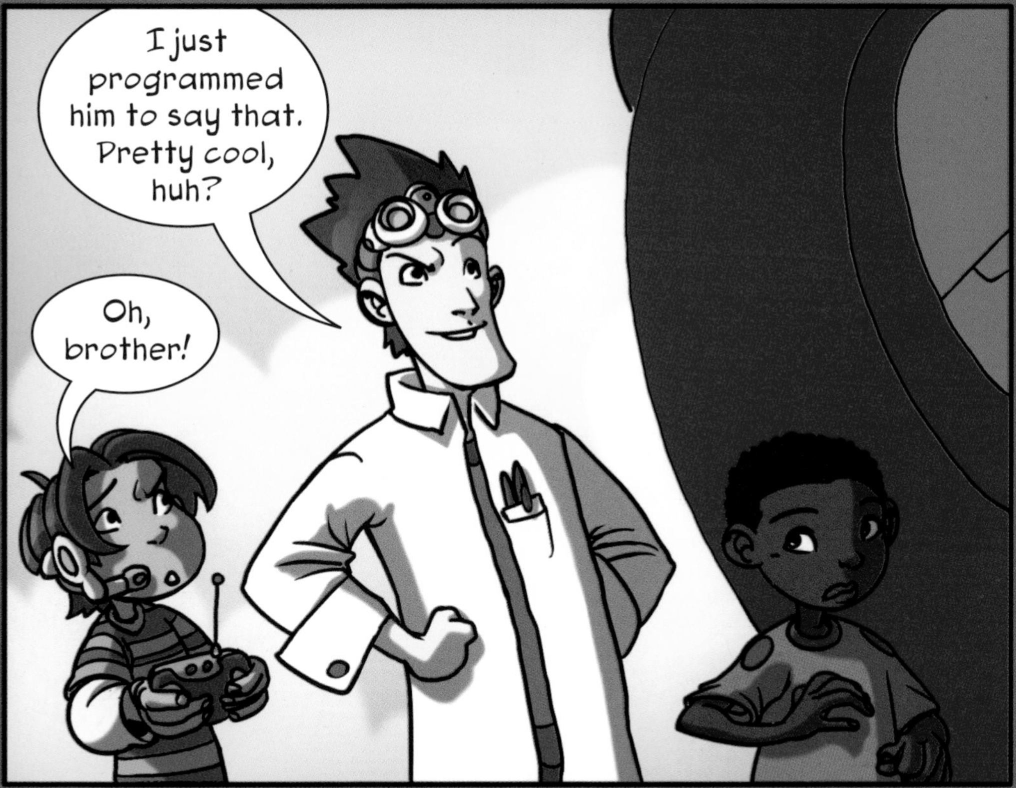
I just programmed him to say that. Pretty cool, huh?
Oh, brother!

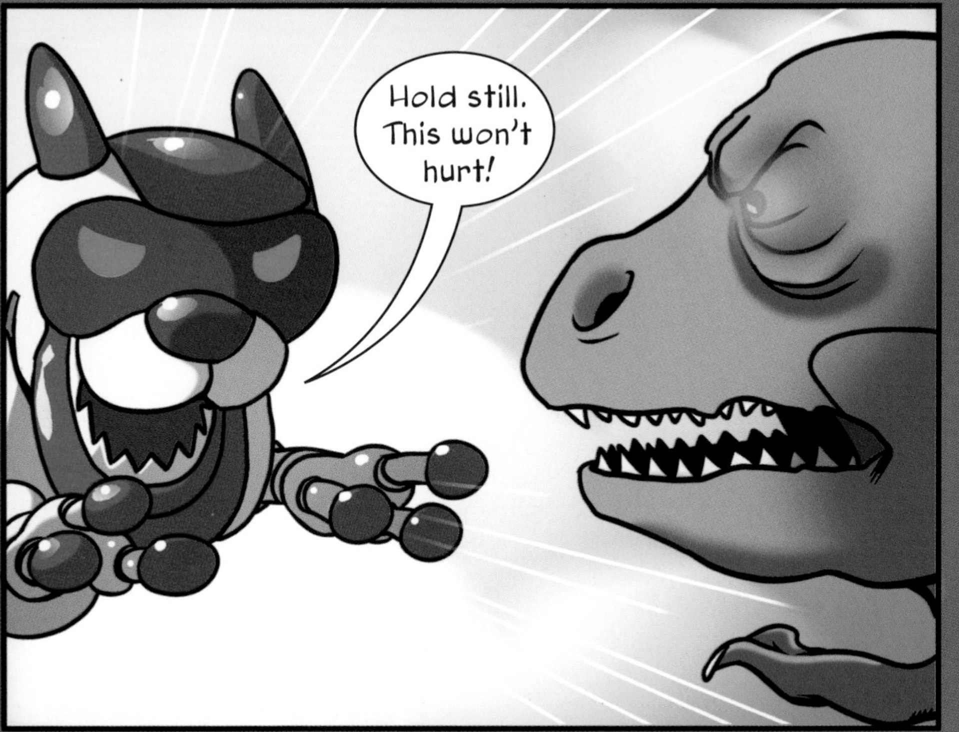
Hold still. This won't hurt!

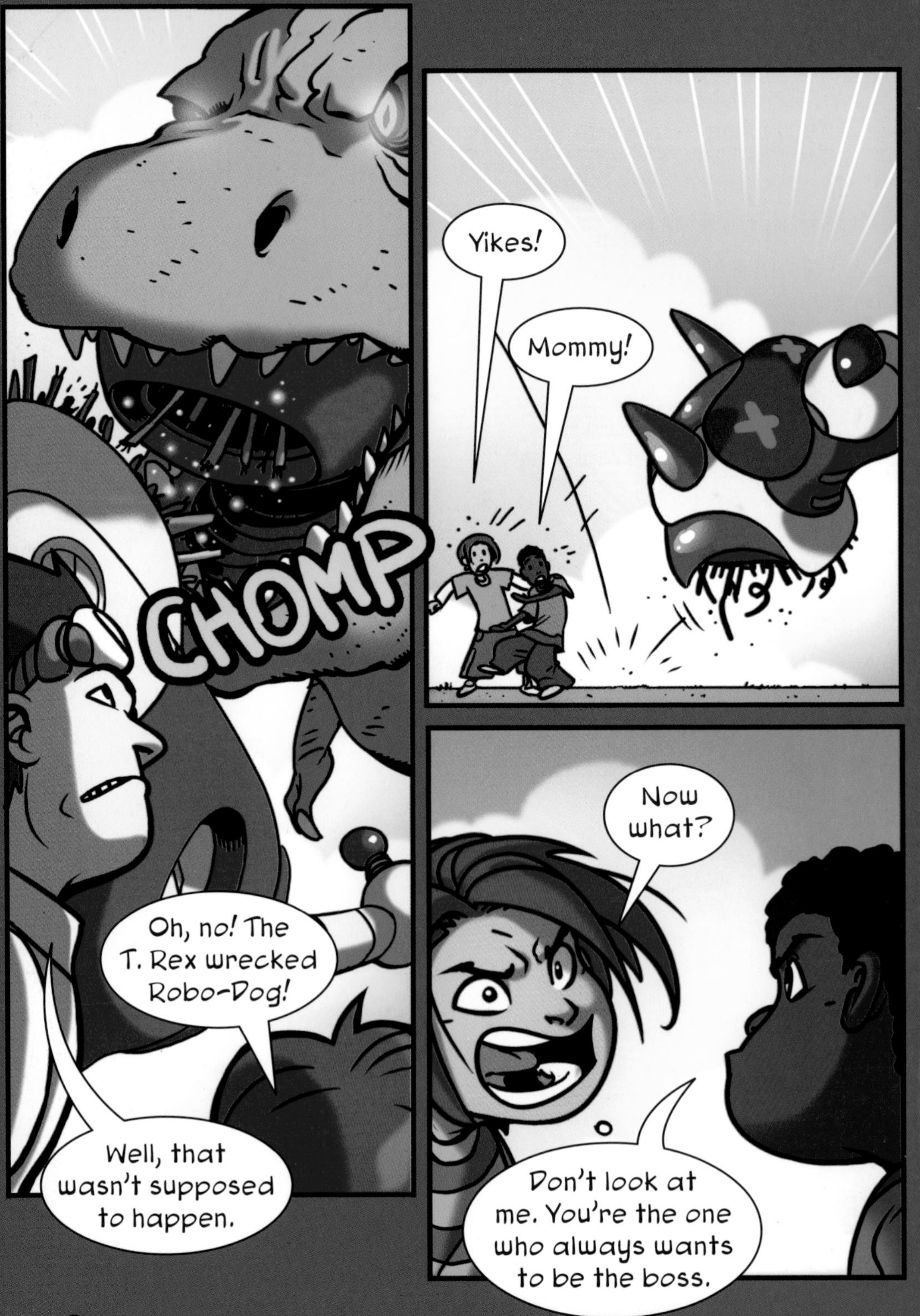
CHOMP
Oh, no! The T. Rex wrecked Robo-Dog!
Well, that wasn't supposed to happen.
Yikes!
Mommy!
Now what?
Don't look at me. You're the one who always wants to be the boss.

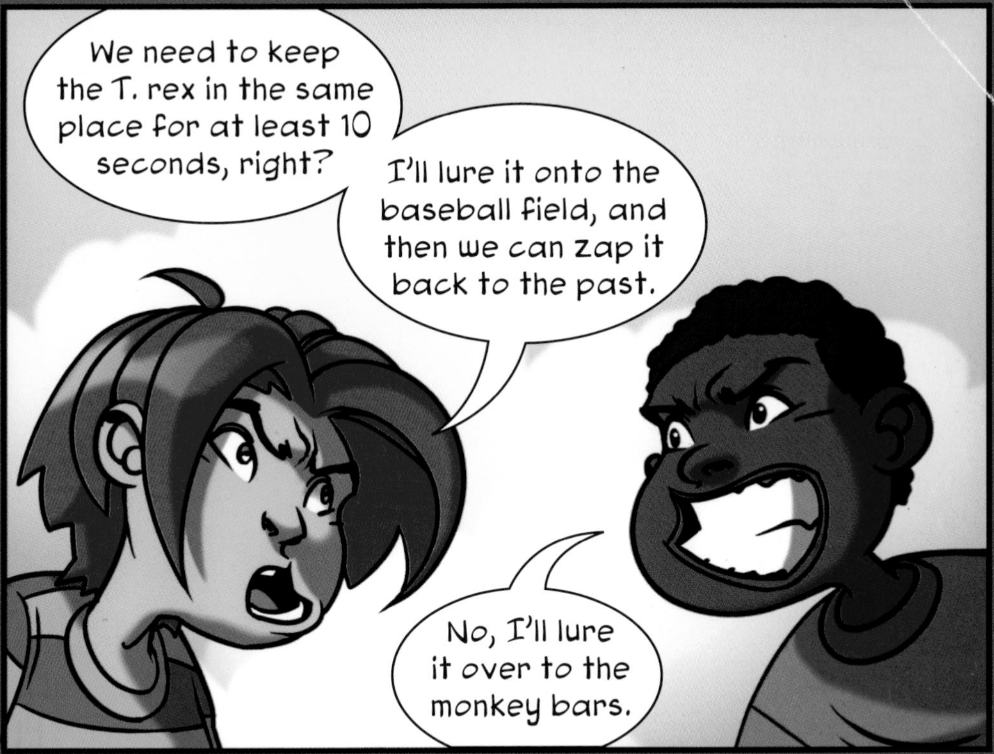
We need to keep the T. rex in the same place for at least 10 seconds, right?
I'll lure it onto the baseball field, and then we can zap it back to the past.
No, I'll lure it over to the monkey bars.

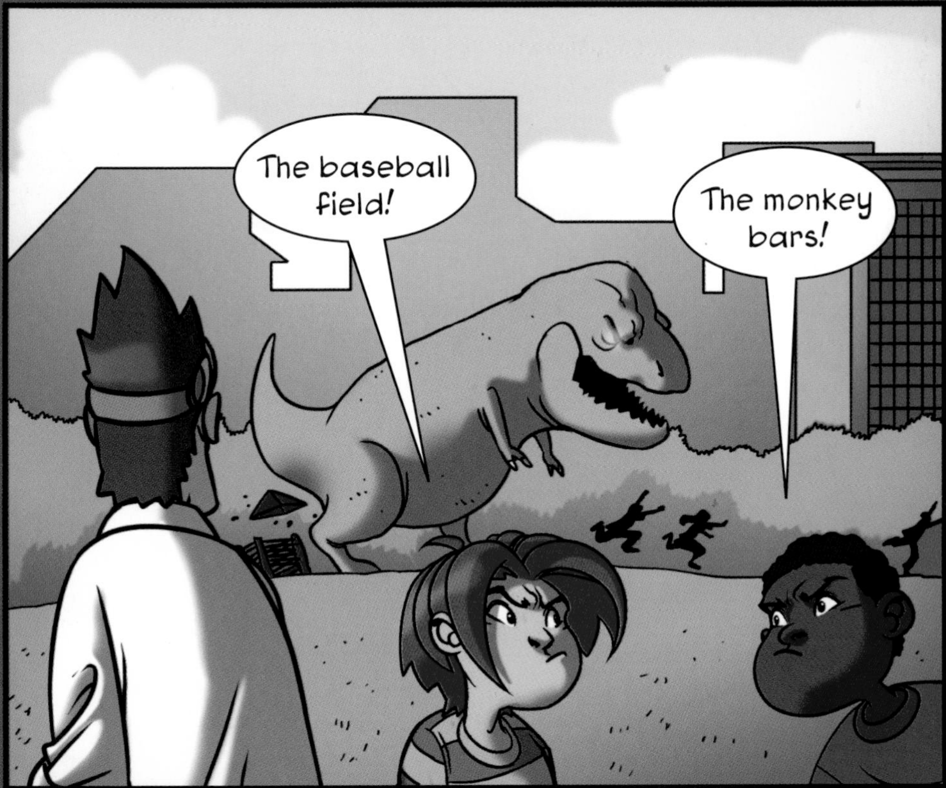
The baseball field!
The monkey bars!

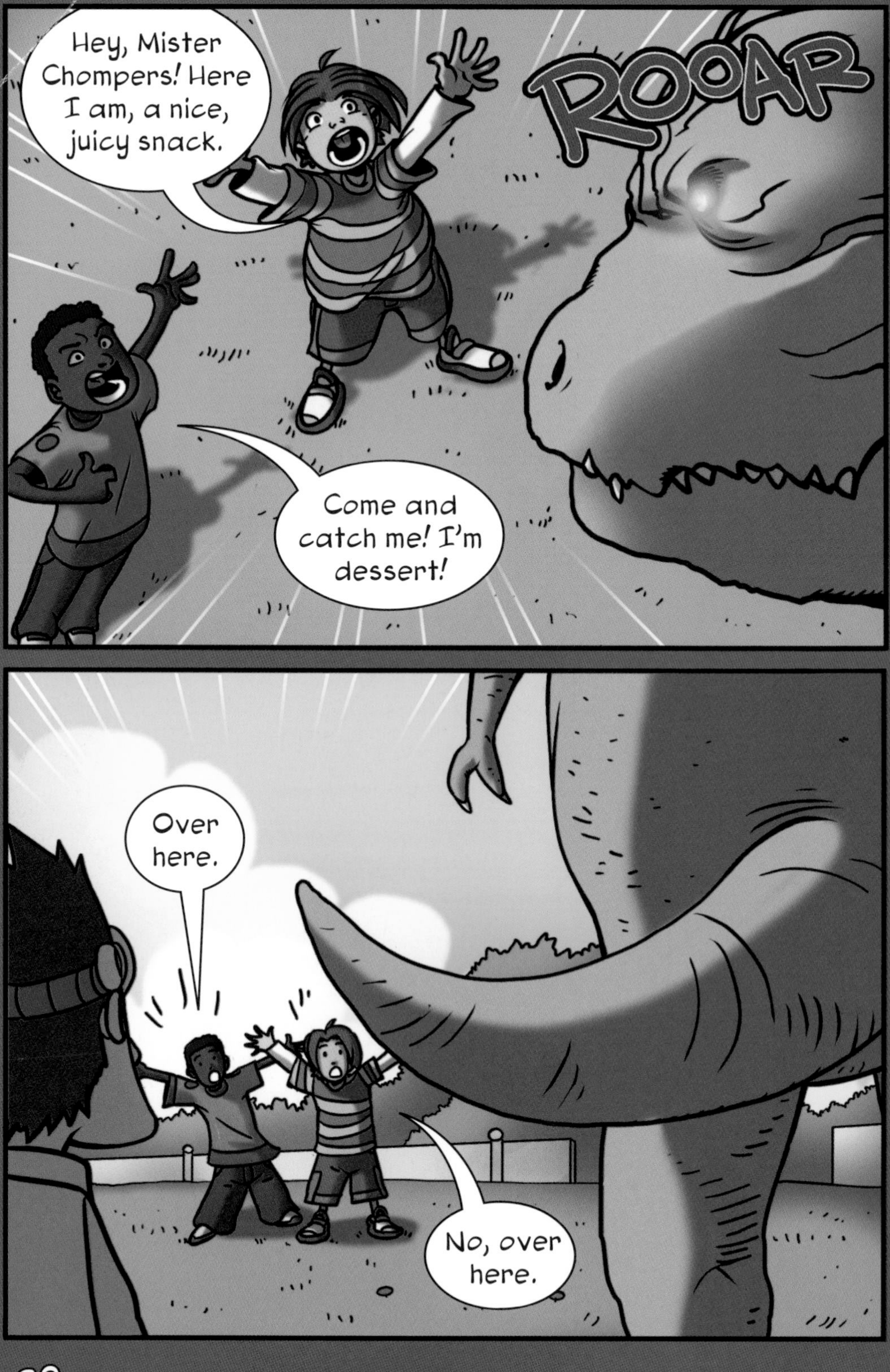
Hey, Mister Chompers! Here I am, a nice, juicy snack.
ROOAR
Come and catch me! I'm dessert!
Over here.
No, over here.

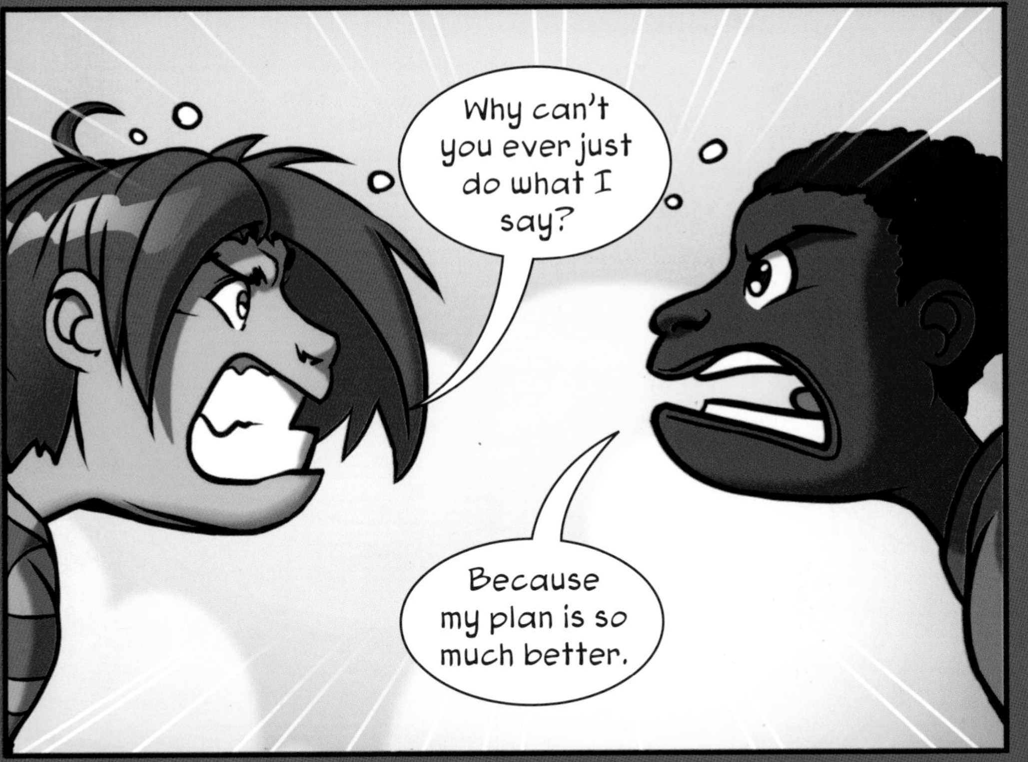
Why can't you ever just do what I say?
Because my plan is so much better.

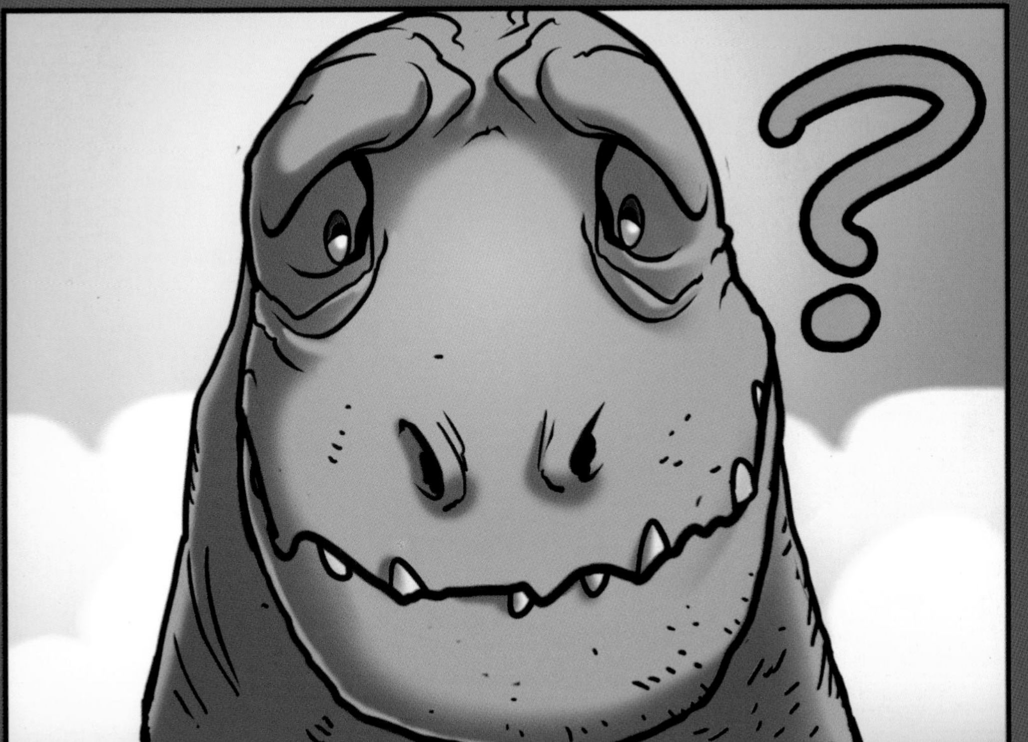
?

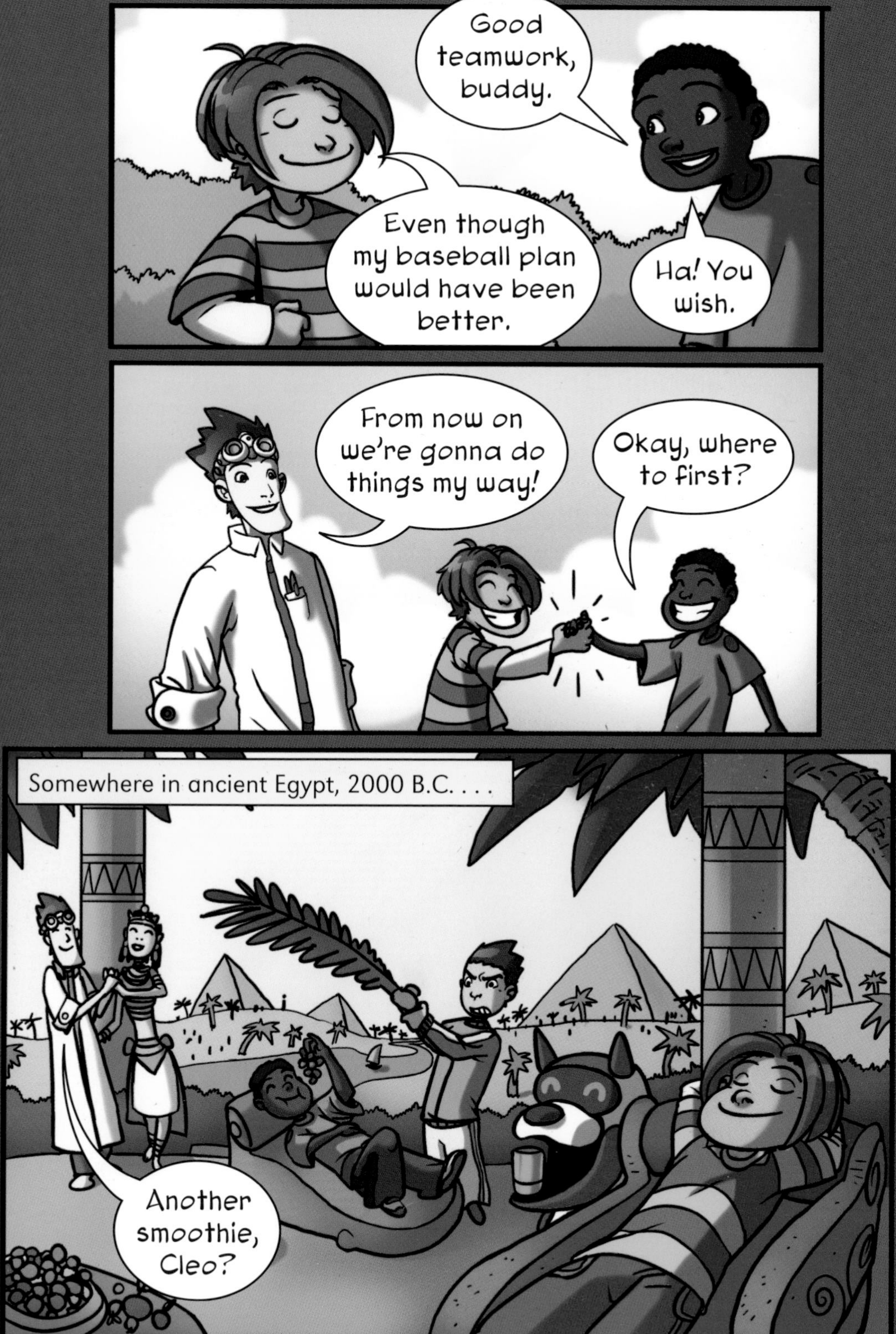
Good teamwork, buddy.
Even though my baseball plan would have been better.
Ha! You wish.
From now on we're gonna do things my way!
Okay, where to first?
Somewhere in ancient Egypt, 2000 B.C. . . .
Another smoothie, Cleo?

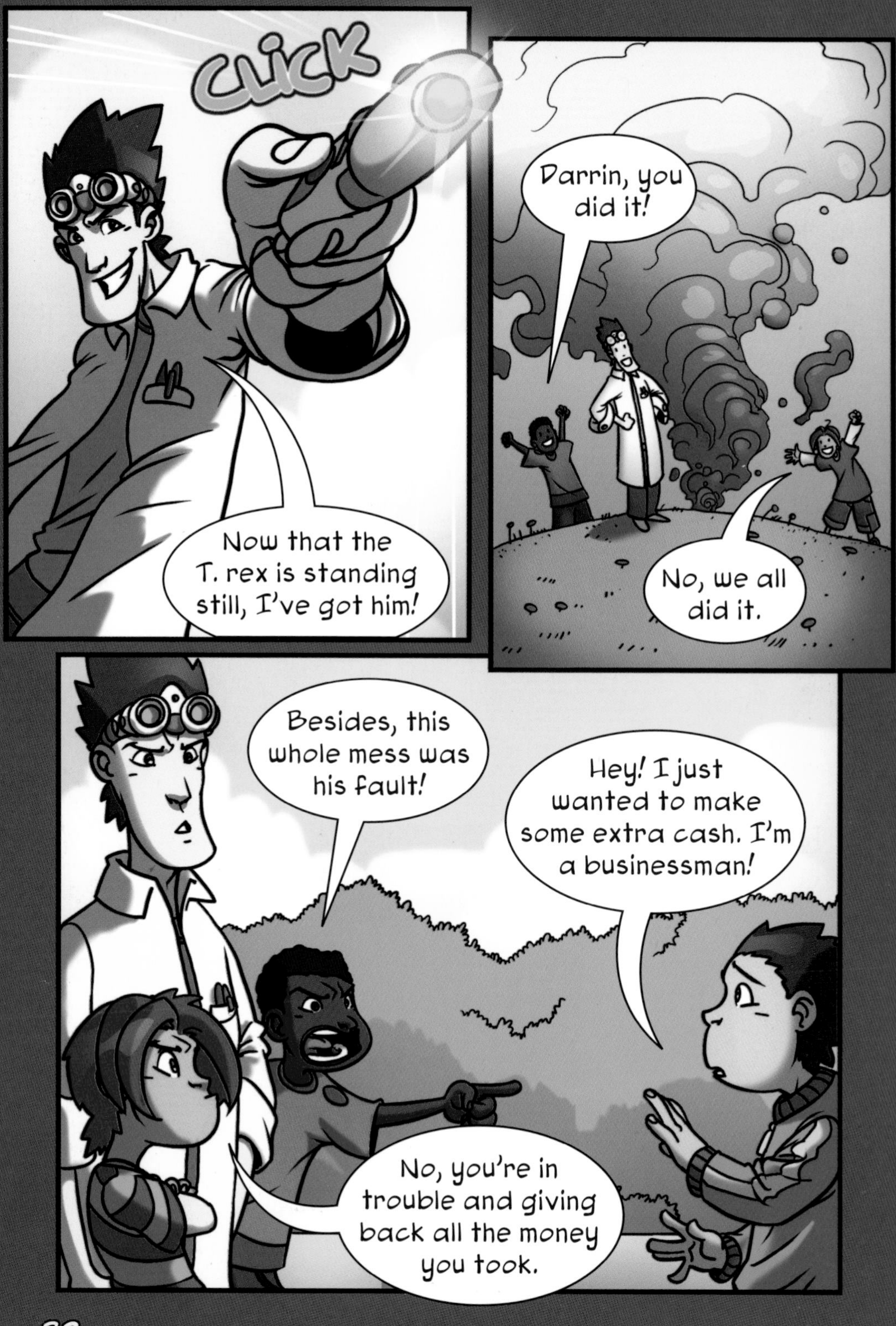
CLICK
Now that the T. rex is standing still, I've got him!
Darrin, you did it!
No, we all did it.
Besides, this whole mess was his fault!
Hey! I just wanted to make some extra cash. I'm a businessman!
No, you're in trouble and giving back all the money you took.

ABOUT THE AUTHOR

Growing up, Scott Nickel wanted to be a comic book writer or a mad scientist. As an adult, he gets to do both. In his secret literary lab, Scott has created more than a dozen graphic novels for Stone Arch Books featuring time travelers, zombies, robots, giant insects, and mutant lunch ladies. Scott's *Night of the Homework Zombies* received the 2007 Golden Duck award for Best Science Fiction Picture Book. When not creating crazy comics, Scott squeezes in a full-time job as a writer and editor at Jim Davis's Garfield studio. He lives in Muncie, Indiana, with his wife, two teenage sons, and an ever-growing number of cats.

ABOUT THE ILLUSTRATOR

Enrique (ehn-REE-kay) Corts became a professional illustrator at age 19, working on short stories for a Spanish comic magazine. After finishing his art studies, he entered the graphic design and advertising world, spending endless hours chained to his computer. Later, he worked as a concept artist in Great Britain on video games such as *Worms 3D, EyeToy Play 3,* and *Play 4.*

Enrique lives in Palma de Mallorca, Spain. Enrique thinks perhaps someday he will go back to his native Valencia in his quest for more sunlight.

GLOSSARY

Cretaceous Period (kri-TAY-shush PIHR-ee-uhd)—a period of time about 144 to 65 million years ago

Egyptian (ee-JIP-shuhn)—often refers to an ancient person from the country of Egypt in northeast Africa

extinct (ek-STINGKT)—something that no longer exists; dinosaurs no longer exist, so they are extinct

herbivores (HUR-buh-vorz)—animals that eat plants for food instead of eating meat

invention (in-VENT-shuhn)—a completely new and original product or idea

Jurassic Age (juh-RA-sik AYJ)—a period of time about 206 to 144 million years ago, when many dinosaurs roamed Earth

PB&J (P B AND J)—slang term for peanut butter and jelly

triceratops (trye-SER-uh-tops)—a large, plant-eating dinosaur with three horns and a fan-shaped collar of bone

tyrannosaurus (ti-RAN-uh-sor-uhs)—a large meat-eating dinosaur that walked on its hind legs, also known as T. rex

MORE ABOUT TYRANNOSAURUS REX

Did you know the scientific name Tyrannosaurus rex (ti-RAN-uh-sor-uhs REX) means "Tyrant Lizard King?" Weighing 5 to 7 tons, this dino certainly was reptile royalty. Here are a few more facts about this giant beast.

The T. rex was the star of the movie *Jurassic Park.* But these dinos didn't actually live during the Jurassic Age. They lived between 65 to 85 million years ago during a time known as the **Cretaceous Period** (kri-TAY-shush PIHR-ee-uhd).

At 40 feet (12 meters) long and 20 feet (6 meters) tall, the T. rex was one of the largest meat-eating dinos.

Although the T. rex was big, that doesn't mean it was slow. Some scientists believe these beasts could chase down their prey at more than 40 miles (64 kilometers) per hour.

For such a large beast, the T. rex's arms were surprisingly small. At only 3 feet (1 meter) long, they were too short to capture prey.

Instead of grabbing prey with its tiny arms, T. rex grabbed food with its teeth. Each T. rex tooth measured more than 9 inches (23 centimeters) long! That's the size of a large banana.

T. rex used its giant teeth to satisfy a giant appetite. With one bite, scientists believe the T. rex could gobble up about 500 pounds of meat. If dinos ate hamburgers, T. rex could have swallowed more than 2,000 in a single bite.

All of the T. rex fossils discovered have been found in North America. In 1990, one of the best-known and most complete skeletons was discovered in South Dakota by fossil hunter Sue Hendrickson. In October 1997, the Field Museum in Chicago, Illinois, bought the bones for a record $8.4 million. The fossil, known simply as "Sue," is now on display for all visitors to look at.

DISCUSSION QUESTIONS

1. Ben took David's time machine controller without permission. If you were David, would you forgive Ben for taking the remote? Why or why not?

2. In the story, Ben and Darrin help David stop the T. rex. Do you think David could have stopped the T. rex by himself? Explain your answer.

3. Do you think making Brendan pay back the money he took is a good punishment? How would you have punished Brendan for bringing back the T. rex?

WRITING PROMPTS

1. Robo-Dog 3000 was a pretty strange pet. Write a story about your favorite pet. If you don't have one, describe your dream pet. Would it be a robot, a wild animal, or something even crazier?

2. If you had a time machine would you travel to the past or the future? Write a story about the places you would go and the adventures you would have.

3. T. rex and the triceratops are just two types of dinosaurs. Ask an adult to help you find information about another dinosaur or extinct animal. Describe what it looked like, where it lived, and what it ate.

INTERNET SITES

The book may be over, but the adventure is just beginning.

Do you want to read more about the subjects or ideas in this book? Want to play cool games or watch videos about the authors who write these books? Then go to FactHound. At *www.facthound.com*, you'll be able to do all that, and more. The FactHound website can also send you to other safe Internet sites.

Check it out!